Something was happening to MacKenzie.

Feeling as if she were free-floating, she realized that her feet were off the ground. Quade had caught her so fast, so hard, he'd raised her off the ground.

Her face was inches from his.

His lips were inches from hers.

And something within her leaped out of nowhere, wanting to close the gap. Begging to close it.

Their eyes met and held as if some force was compelling them to look at one another, unable to look away, unable to look anywhere else.

She wanted him to kiss her.

He was no one to her and she no one to him, but she wanted him to kiss her. Right now, more than anything in the world, she wanted to feel desirable.

Wanted to feel something for someone…

Dear Reader,

Most of us look forward to October for the end-of-the-month treats, but we here at Silhouette Special Edition want you to experience those treats all month long—beginning, this time around, with the next book in our MOST LIKELY TO... series. In *The Pregnancy Project* by Victoria Pade, a woman who's used to getting what she wants, wants a baby. And the man she's earmarked to help her is her arrogant ex-classmate, now a brilliant, if brash, fertility expert.

Popular author Gina Wilkins brings back her acclaimed FAMILY FOUND series with *Adding to the Family,* in which a party girl turned single mother of twins needs help—and her handsome accountant *(accountant?),* a single father himself, is just the one to give it. In *She's Having a Baby,* bestselling author Marie Ferrarella continues her miniseries, THE CAMEO, with this story of a vivacious, single, pregnant woman and her devastatingly handsome—if reserved—next-door neighbor. Special Edition welcomes author Brenda Harlen and her poignant novel *Once and Again,* a heartwarming story of homecoming and second chances. *About the Boy* by Sharon DeVita is the story of a beautiful single mother, a widowed chief of police...and a matchmaking little boy. And Silhouette is thrilled to have *Blindsided* by talented author Leslie LaFoy in our lineup. When a woman who's inherited a hockey team decides that they need the best coach in the business, she applies to a man who thought he'd put his hockey days behind him. But he's been...blindsided!

So enjoy, be safe and come back in November for more. This is my favorite time of year (well, the beginning of it, anyway).

Regards,

Gail Chasan
Senior Editor

Please address questions and book requests to:
Silhouette Reader Service
U.S.: 3010 Walden Ave., P.O. Box 1325, Buffalo, NY 14269
Canadian: P.O. Box 609, Fort Erie, Ont. L2A 5X3

MARIE FERRARELLA

SHE'S HAVING A BABY

SPECIAL EDITION®

Published by Silhouette Books

America's Publisher of Contemporary Romance

To Charlie, because I still believe in magic, and you.

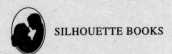 SILHOUETTE BOOKS

ISBN 0-373-24713-3

SHE'S HAVING A BABY

Copyright © 2005 by Marie Rydzynski-Ferrarella

This edition published by arrangement with Harlequin Books S.A.

® and TM are trademarks of Harlequin Books S.A., used under license.
Trademarks indicated with ® are registered in the United States Patent
and Trademark Office, the Canadian Trade Marks Office and in other
countries.

Visit Silhouette Books at www.eHarlequin.com

Printed in U.S.A.

Books by Marie Ferrarella

ChildFinders, Inc.
A Hero for All Seasons IM #932
A Forever Kind of Hero IM #943
Hero in the Nick of Time IM #956
Hero for Hire IM #1042
An Uncommon Hero Silhouette Books
A Hero in Her Eyes IM #1059
Heart of a Hero IM #1105

Baby's Choice
Caution: Baby Ahead SR #1007
Mother on the Wing SR #1026
Baby Times Two SR #1037

The Baby of the Month Club
Baby's First Christmas SE #997
Happy New Year—Baby! IM #686
The 7lb., 2oz. Valentine Yours Truly
Husband: Optional SD #988
Do You Take This Child? SR #1145
Detective Dad World's Most
  Eligible Bachelors
The Once and Future Father IM #1017
In the Family Way Silhouette Books
Baby Talk Silhouette Books
An Abundance of Babies SE #1422

Like Mother, Like Daughter
One Plus One Makes Marriage SR #1328
Never Too Late for Love SR #1351

The Bachelors of Blair Memorial
In Graywolf's Hands IM #1155
M.D. Most Wanted IM #1167
Mac's Bedside Manner SE #1492
Undercover M.D. IM #1191
The M.D.'s Surprise Family IM #1653

Two Halves of a Whole
The Baby Came C.O.D. SR #1264
Desperately Seeking Twin Yours Truly

*The Reeds
Callaghan's Way IM #601
Serena McKee's Back in Town IM #808

The Cameo
Because a Husband Is Forever SE #1671
She's Having a Baby SE #1713

*Unflashed series

Those Sinclairs
Holding Out for a Hero IM #496
Heroes Great and Small IM #501
Christmas Every Day IM #538
Caitlin's Guardian Angel IM #661

The Cutlers of the Shady Lady Ranch
(Yours Truly titles)
Fiona and the Sexy Stranger
Cowboys Are for Loving
Will and the Headstrong Female
The Law and Ginny Marlow
A Match for Morgan
A Triple Threat to Bachelorhood SR #1564

*McClellans & Marinos
Man Trouble SR #815
The Taming of the Teen SR #839
Babies on His Mind SR #920
The Baby Beneath the Mistletoe SR #1408

*The Alaskans
Wife in the Mail SE #1217
Stand-In Mom SE #1294
Found: His Perfect Wife SE #1310
The M.D. Meets His Match SE #1401
Lily and the Lawman SE #1467
The Bride Wore Blue Jeans SE #1565

*The Pendletons
Baby in the Middle SE #892
Husband: Some Assembly Required SE #931

The Mom Squad
A Billionaire and a Baby SE #1528
A Bachelor and a Baby SD #1503
The Baby Mission IM #1220
Beauty and the Baby SR #1668

Cavanaugh Justice
Racing Against Time IM #1249
Crime and Passion IM #1256
Internal Affair Silhouette Books
Dangerous Games IM #1274
The Strong Silent Type SE #1613
Cavanaugh's Woman SE #1617
In Broad Daylight IM #1315
Alone in the Dark IM #1327
Dangerous Disguise IM #1339

MARIE FERRARELLA

This RITA® Award-winning author has written over one hundred and forty books for Silhouette, some under the name Marie Nicole. Her romances are beloved by fans worldwide.

Prologue

June 1, 1864

Amanda Deveaux closed her hand around the cameo. For three years now she'd worn it, never removing it from her neck. She'd promised to wear it until he returned to claim her for his wife. The cameo had become her own personal badge of courage. Embossed on the delicate Wedgwood blue oval was the profile of a young Greek woman, carved in ivory. Penelope, waiting for her Ulysses to come home to her.

Just as she was waiting for her Will to come home to her. Will, who had asked her to wait for him. Will, who had promised to return, no matter how low the fortunes of this miserable, misbegotten war between the states laid him.

He'd sworn it and she'd believed him. She *still* believed. Because Lieutenant William Slattery had never lied to her.

They had known each other from childhood. Loved one another since childhood. Will had withstood her mother's sly, cutting remarks and her father's sharp, delving scrutiny because Will's people were not as rich as hers. He'd put up with both parents because he'd loved her. He'd been her brother Jonathan's best friend. Jonathan, who was gone now, one of the brave who had fallen at Chancelorsville.

At least they knew Jonathan's fate. She didn't know Will's.

There'd been no word from Will since Gettysburg. Not since his name had been listed among those who were missing.

These days, her heart felt leaden within her breast. It was hard clinging to hope all this time, hard holding her breath as she looked down the long road leading back to her family's plantation, now all but in ruins, waiting for him to ride up. Just as he'd promised he would.

"It's a sin, wasting away like that over a man who was only two steps removed from white trash."

Coming out onto the decaying porch, Belinda Deveaux looked accusingly at her older daughter. Her oldest child now that Jonathan was in his grave. She raised her head, anger and impatience permanently etched into a face that had once been regarded as the most beautiful in three counties.

Her small lips pursed. "Frasier O'Brien would marry you."

Amanda's eyes widened in surprise. Frasier O'Brien had returned from the war—some said he had deserted—to take over his ailing father's emporium. Shrewd and always able to turn a situation to his advantage, Frasier had found a way to turn a healthy profit in the midst of a time beset with need and despair. He was easily now the richest man in the county. And her mother clearly favored him. Money had always drawn her mother's attention.

"Frasier is Savannah's intended. He's asked for her hand in marriage," she reminded her mother, indignant for her younger sister.

"Yes, but he wants you," her mother told her, a dark knowledge in her eyes. "This could be your last chance to marry, girl. Think. You're almost twenty-one. If you do not marry Frasier, what will become of you?"

"Don't worry about me, Mother. Worry about Savannah, who, according to you, is engaged to a man whose heart she doesn't possess."

"I *do* worry about you," her mother reiterated. "I worry about you because you, my empty-headed daughter, are in love with a dead man."

Anger flared in Amanda's breast. "Will is not dead," she cried. "If he were dead, I would know it, Mother. I would feel it inside. Here, where my heart is." She struck her breast like an penitent sinner asking for forgiveness. "I would know. But he's coming back to me. He promised."

Belinda drew herself up. Small, gaunt and draped in black since Jonathan's death, the woman resembled a wraith.

"William Slattery is dead," she pronounced. "As dead as your brother and the sooner you realize that, the sooner you will come back to your senses."

Amanda walked away from her mother. Away from the house that was so badly in the need of care. Away to wait by the side of the road the way she did every day.

"Wait for me," Will had whispered before he'd released her from their last embrace. And she would, because she was his. Forever. And nothing would change that.

Chapter One

Present Day

"**Y**ou're glowing! My God, you're really glowing. Do you realize you're glowing? I had no idea that was actually possible. Pablo, I don't want you to touch her with your makeup brush. Nothing you can do would improve on this look. Is our camera set for 'glow'?"

The last question was fired over assistant producer MacKenzie Ryan's shoulder in the general direction of the set where their afternoon show *...And Now a Word from Dakota* was being shot. The rest of the words rushing out of MacKenzie's mouth as she quickly crossed the threshold into Dakota Delaney's dressing room were aimed directly at her best friend.

Offstage, the latter's name was now officially Dakota Delaney Russell due to her recent marriage to Ian Russell. The star of the popular daytime talk show had just returned from her two-week honeymoon and the only one who had missed Dakota more than her audience was MacKenzie.

To her left, MacKenzie was aware that the tall, gaunt makeup artist who insisted on being called Pablo was scowling at her for preventing him from doing his work. For the moment, she ignored him. It wasn't as if Dakota were one of those people who needed much makeup anyway. Fresh-faced, she was still drop-dead gorgeous.

Battling another annoying wave of queasiness, MacKenzie forced a grin to her face, aimed at the woman with whom she had once shared dreams and a dorm room. She pushed a strand of strawberry-blond hair out of her eyes. "It has been absolute hell without you, Dakota. I hate working with guest hosts. They're so not you."

Dakota shifted around in her seat to face her best friend. "Nice to be missed."

"Missed?" MacKenzie echoed with a hoot. "If you'd called to say you were extending your honeymoon with that hunk of a man you landed for another week, I would have put my head in the oven."

Pablo shot her a look that swept over her five-foot-three body swiftly and critically. "You're small enough for all of you to fit in the oven."

The comment was punctuated with a haughty snap of his wrists as he closed the lid down on his huge makeup case. Pablo had just taken over for the previous head makeup artist, Albert Hamlin, who had been moved to a prime-time talk show. Today would have marked the first time he'd worked on Dakota, although he had the opportunity to apply makeup to the various guest stars who had temporarily helmed the show. It was evident that Pablo didn't like limits being imposed on his work.

Dakota offered the temperamental man a conciliatory smile. "Maybe just some lip liner," she suggested.

Pablo sighed dramatically and opened the case again. "Whatever you wish, Ms. Delaney." After finding the shade Dakota favored, he held the wand out to her.

Unable to hold back any longer, MacKenzie moved the man aside in order to hug not the star of the fan-favorite program, but her best friend. The woman she still turned to in the middle of her best moments, as well as her worst.

Right now, it was the latter, but this was no time to share.

The embrace was warm and enthusiastic.

"Was it wonderful?" she asked, releasing Dakota. "Tell me it was wonderful." MacKenzie sighed, for one moment taking a mental journey back to their college days when they had sat up until the small hours of the morning, talking about their dates. Life was a great deal simpler back then. All you had to worry about were grades and trying not to break out before a date. "I need daydreams and I haven't any of my own."

"That's because you don't have a life," Pablo said under his breath but audibly enough for the man in the

hall changing the lightbulb in the ceiling to hear. The
latter chuckled.

MacKenzie spared Pablo a dirty look, but made no
protest. That was because what he said was true. She
didn't have a life—at least, not a social one. Since her
promotion to assistant producer, all of five days ago, she
had decided to dedicate herself to the task of oversee-
ing every aspect of the program. It was the kind of job
that didn't end when she pulled out of the parking lot
late at night.

But it wasn't just her newly attained position, that
was responsible for her not having a life. She didn't
have a social life by choice. Because the life she'd been
leading up until a few weeks ago had blown up in her
face. Her heart broken, she was not about to go back
into the dating pool and lay herself open to endure another possible mishap.

It bothered MacKenzie no end to discover that she
wasn't as resilient as she'd thought she was, but there
you had it. She wasn't and she was just going to have
to learn how to live with that instead of some kind, loving, mythical male who didn't exist except perhaps in
the pages of a script.

Accepting the lipstick that Pablo held out to her,
Dakota applied the soft pink shade to her lips herself. The
natural energy that had been the hallmark of Dakota's life
since she'd first met her seemed to be hyped up by several amps, MacKenzie noticed. Or maybe that was just because she felt pale in comparison to her friend. It seemed
like she was tired all the time now, like an old-fashioned
clock that couldn't be fully wound up anymore.

Of course, there was a reason for that, she thought darkly.

Dakota handed the lipstick back to Pablo and turned in her chair to face MacKenzie. She studied her friend's face for a moment. Concern nibbled at the outer edges of her consciousness. "Pablo, would you mind leaving us alone for a few minutes?"

The man's dark head popped up, his black eyes alert. "Girl talk?" Pablo pouted at the exclusion. "I have as much right to listen to girl talk as the nex— Oh, all right," he huffed. He hefted his makeup case, a tiny muscle defining itself in his thin arm as it strained under the weight. "I know when I'm not wanted."

MacKenzie closed her eyes and shook her head as Pablo exited the room. He closed the door behind him with an audible jolt that all but shook the door frame. She sighed. "He has gotten so temperamental since his promotion."

Dakota had no desire to talk about the makeup artist. Her thoughts were all centered on her friend. She rose to her feet, taking MacKenzie's hands into hers. "Speaking of promotions, Zee, I heard that they made you assistant producer."

MacKenzie shrugged off the honor disparagingly. "Yeah, they did."

Dakota couldn't resist hugging the other woman. The top of MacKenzie's head came up to her chin. "God, I am so proud of you."

MacKenzie struggled to block out another wave of queasiness that threatened to overwhelm her. Mind over matter, Zee, mind over matter, she kept repeating fiercely.

"Forget me, look at you." Stepping back, she looked at Dakota again. "Married. Glowing."

Dakota laughed, sitting down in the chair again. Her eyes shone as she thought of Ian. "He does have that effect on me." She wasn't aware of the sigh that escaped her lips, but MacKenzie was. "Love is really, really wonderful—" She stopped abruptly and looked at MacKenzie sharply, suspicion entering her eyes. "Speaking of which, how are you and Jeff—or shouldn't I ask?"

The shrug was evasive. Hapless. She knew she didn't have a prayer of fooling Dakota. Nor did she really want to. It was just that saying the words hurt. "I'm fine. Jeff's fine."

Dakota's eyes narrowed. They'd been friends since college and no one could read the diminutive, bubbly woman like she could. The conclusion wasn't difficult to reach. "But you're not fine together."

"No," MacKenzie sighed. Two weeks and she still felt as if she were juggling hot coals bare-handed whenever she thought about the breakup. He'd been kind, trying so hard not to hurt her. As if that were possible, given how she'd initially felt.

She wanted to hate him, but she couldn't. She could only grieve. "We're not together. He's together with his wife."

Dakota's mouth dropped open. This was new. "His wife?"

MacKenzie laughed dryly. The sound rang hollow in

the small dressing room. "Yeah, a little detail he forgot to mention."

Dakota could only shake her head, clearly stunned. "He's married?"

"Separated at the time, so he said. But yes, married." Afraid she would see pity in Dakota's eyes, she squared her shoulders the way she'd often seen her friend do and raised her chin. It was purely a defensive move. "And out of my life."

For a moment, their eyes met and held. In short order, Dakota made up her mind. Leaning her head forward just slightly in order to get her hair off her neck, she located the small knot that held the two velvet ends of her necklace together and undid it.

Watching, MacKenzie frowned. "Dakota, what are you doing?"

Removing her necklace, Dakota held it up in front of her friend. On the end of the velvet ribbon was the cameo she had purchased at an antique shop in upstate New York. The cameo she firmly believed with all her heart had brought her and Ian Russell together in the first place. The cameo came along with a legend.

"I'm taking the cameo off so that I can give it to you."

"Dakota—" MacKenzie began to protest, shaking her head.

She was about to step back, but Dakota was faster. The latter took her hand and turned it so that her palm was facing up. Dakota laid the cameo across it. She vividly remembered that the woman who had sold her the necklace had said that once she'd felt its magic, once true love had entered her life, she was charged with passing the necklace on to someone else who was in need of its magic. Someone like her best friend.

"I've felt the effects of its magic. Now it's your turn."

MacKenzie stared at her, dumbfounded. Dakota had been valedictorian in their graduating class. "You don't really believe—"

"Oh, yes, I do," Dakota cut in adamantly. "I'm not much on legends and magic, but this worked just the way I was told it would." Seeing the skepticism in MacKenzie's eyes, Dakota pressed on. She had once been a disbeliever herself. "The woman in the antique store told me that the legend went that whoever wore the cameo would have their true love enter their life."

"Dakota, we're New Yorkers now. We're too sophisticated for that." Although part of her wished she could believe in magic. In happily-ever-afters and men who loved to their last dying breath. But she was too old to hang onto illusions. There came a time to grow up. "That's hype and you know it."

"No," Dakota contradicted firmly, "I don't. What I know is that when I put it on, I met Ian that same afternoon. Maybe it's crazy," she allowed, "but there is no other explanation for it than magic. When I went back to talk to that old woman in the antique shop, the owner said no one matching her description worked there. Except that I *did* talk to her. I *did* see her.

"And she looked exactly like the photograph he had hanging on his wall of his great-great-aunt—the same great-aunt whose funeral was taking place the day I bought the cameo from her." It sounded fantastic and she would have been the first to doubt the story if she hadn't lived through it herself. "Now, if that's not magic, I don't know what is."

MacKenzie looked at the necklace. The cameo was a woman's profile, carved in ivory and delicately set against a Wedgwood blue background. It was a beautiful piece, but only jewelry, not a cure for a broken heart. "I don't believe in magic."

Dakota placed her hand over MacKenzie's in mute comfort. "You did, once."

MacKenzie drew her hand away, determined to brazen it out. "I also believed in Santa Claus, once. But I grew up."

The woman in the shop hadn't said that belief was an integral part of the experience. "Okay, you don't have to believe, you just have to wear it." She looked at MacKenzie, mutely supplicating. "What do you have to lose?"

MacKenzie laughed shortly. "The cameo, for one." She looked down at the cameo and shook her head. "You know how bad I am about things like that. I'd feel awful if I lost it." She attempted to push the piece back into Dakota's hand.

But Dakota merely pushed it back toward her instead. "Then don't lose it," she advised. "Wear it. As a favor to me, Zee," she added, her eyes locking with MacKenzie's again.

MacKenzie could feel herself wearing down. It wasn't that she didn't like the cameo. It was beautiful and she would have loved to wear it. But she also knew that there was no magic in it. Magic was for the very young and the very old to believe in. And the very superstitious. That wasn't her. "Waste of time."

The argument was unacceptable. Dakota shrugged it off. "Time goes by anyway."

Outflanked, MacKenzie surrendered. "God, but you are chipper, even for you."

"I know." Her smile fairly lit up the entire room, with light to spare. "I feel like I'm floating."

It had to be wonderful to feel that way, MacKenzie thought. "Try not to levitate until after the show, okay?"

"Deal." Dakota looked down at the cameo pointedly. "If you—"

"Wear the necklace—yes, I know. Way ahead of you on that one." She sighed, capitulating. "Okay, I'll wear it."

Dakota kept looking at her expectantly. Waiting. "Now."

MacKenzie glanced at her watch. It was almost time to go on. "Dakota—"

Dakota rose from her seat, moving around to stand behind MacKenzie. She reached around her, her hand out for the cameo that was nestled in MacKenzie's hand. "Now," she repeated.

With a sigh, MacKenzie relinquished the cameo she'd meant to stash in her tiny jewelry box, and placed the piece and its velvet ribbon in her friend's hand. "It's not going to do any good."

"Humor me."

MacKenzie suppressed another sigh. "Okay, you're the star."

"No," Dakota corrected, securing the ribbon and then coming around to take a look at her handiwork. "I'm the friend."

* * *

MacKenzie knew that Dakota meant well. That the woman who had come up the ranks right along with her only had her best interests at heart. But at this point in the game, her own interests were going to have to take a time-out and slip into the back seat.

At least her romantic interests.

She had a career to worry about, granted, but more important than that, she had a brand new life to worry about. The brand new life she'd just discovered yesterday morning existed within her.

Apparently, Jeff was never going to be permanently out of her life.

Or at least a part of him wasn't going to be.

She was pregnant. Probably not more than a few weeks because that was the last time she and Jeff had made love. Three and a half weeks. Just before Dakota's autumn wedding.

Damn it, how could this have happened? Science had advanced so far, you'd think there could be a hundred-percent guarantee for things like birth control pills. But there wasn't because she had used birth-control and still she found herself unexpectedly carrying a new life within her. A baby who by all rights shouldn't have been there.

But it was, she thought, placing her hand over what was an absolutely flat stomach.

It was there. Six stupid sticks, all pointing to the same thing, couldn't be wrong no matter how much she wanted them to be.

Six, that was how many kits she'd brought home,

buying each one at a different drugstore so that if for some reason one batch had emerged from the manufacturer with some kind of malfunction, she could turn to another for the true results.

She'd turned six times.

Not a single one of them had given her a smattering of hope. Each one had pointed to the same results: She was pregnant.

Dragging herself out of her shower this morning after allowing the hot water to wash over her for longer than usual, MacKenzie knew she was going to have to make an appointment with her gynecologist for a true confirmation. Not that she held any real hope that the six sticks had lied to her.

Friday, she thought, drying herself off and then discarding the towel. She'd make the appointment for Friday. Or maybe even sometime next week. Right now, she was too busy with the show.

The show. Oh God, she was going to have to hustle, she thought without glancing at either one of the clocks in her bedroom. She could feel the minutes slipping away.

MacKenzie hurried into her clothes, putting on a straight forest-green skirt and a pale green sweater. Both felt loose. How much longer was that going to last, she wondered. Indefinitely, if the first ten minutes of her day were any indication. She'd spent them throwing up, entering that state while she was still half-asleep. She'd spent the next ten trying to get her bearings, succeeding only marginally.

About to dash out of her apartment, MacKenzie realized that she'd left the cameo behind. She was tempted to keep walking, but she knew that would hurt Dakota's feelings and she didn't want to do that. Besides, she certainly didn't believe in the legend, but the small oval piece of jewelry really was lovely.

Securing the ends together at the nape of her neck, she stood for a moment looking at it.

Nothing.

"Magic, huh?" she scoffed. Lightning certainly wasn't striking. It wasn't even tingling. Still, the cameo did look as if it belonged exactly where it was.

Patting it, she left the room, muttering under her breath about superstitions. Sure, she'd been all for it when Dakota had first appeared on the set wearing it. And, admittedly, she'd been charmed by the idea that a Southern belle had once worn it. But that had been when it had hung around Dakota's neck.

Having it now around her own made her uneasy. Uneasy because she was afraid that despite everything she said to the contrary, she might allow herself to buy into the story. To hope when every logical fiber in her body told her that there was nothing to hope on. That hope itself was only a fabrication.

She wasn't the type that had legends come true.

Crossing the kitchen, MacKenzie glanced at her watch and then bit back an exasperated oath.

How had the time managed to melt away like that? She had less than half an hour to get to the studio and traffic was a bear. It was one of the givens living in New York City. Night or day, traffic was always a force to be reckoned with. A force that usually won.

Why was it that time only seem to lengthen itself when she was alone in bed at night, wondering about the direction of her life? Acutely aware of the fact that the place next to her was empty and would undoubtedly remain that way?

Philosophy later. Hurry now, she counseled herself as she headed for the door. There was no time for breakfast. Just as well. She wasn't sure if her stomach could hold it down. Putting on her shoes and grabbing her oversize purse that held half her life in it, MacKenzie flew out of her Queens garden apartment and to her carport.

Where she came to an abrupt, grinding halt. She wasn't going anywhere.

There was one of those self-rental moving trucks blocking her car, its nose protruding so that it was in the way of the car next to hers, as well. The truck's back doors were both hanging open, displaying its contents for any passersby to see. Normally a curious person, MacKenzie had no interest in the truck's contents. What interested her was the person who belonged to said possessions and said truck.

And he or she was nowhere in sight.

Exasperated, feeling the minutes physically ticking by, MacKenzie fisted her hands on her hips, the loop of her purse slung over her wrist.

She looked back and forth down the length of the carports. "Damn it," she exclaimed audibly.

"Something wrong?"

The deep voice behind her sounded like something that had to be raised by bucket out of the depths of a fifty-foot well. Startled, MacKenzie jumped and swung around, her wide purse swinging an eighth of a beat behind her. Coming around like an afterthought, it hit the person belonging to the baritone voice squarely in the groin.

MacKenzie managed to turn in time to see a giant of a man—he was at least a foot taller than her five-foot-three stature—doubling over, his handsome, rugged face turning from tan to something akin to ash-gray. His deep green eyes were watering.

The horror of what she'd just done and the way he had to be feeling slammed into her. "Oh, my God, I'm sorry. Is there anything I can do?" MacKenzie cried.

"You can back off," Quade Preston ground out the words as he tried to regain both his breath and his composure. Both seemed to be just a step out of reach at the moment. He struggled to overtake them.

"Oh, right, sure." MacKenzie moved back, her eyes wide as she stared at him.

She felt like David the moment after he had brought Goliath down to his knees, except that in this case it had been purely unintentional. If there was anyone she would have wanted to take aim at in this fashion, it was Jeff, even though she knew that wasn't exactly fair. Jeff had never promised her the moon—or tomorrow. She had just assumed…

Lately, her emotions felt as if they were strapped to a roller-coaster ride. This tiny seed inside of her had had terrible repercussions on her emotional state. Right now, she felt like laughing and crying, knowing that neither was acceptable.

Especially laughing.

"I can get ice," she offered, thinking back to when she'd been a kid and her brother Donald had had something similar happen to him. Her father had immediately applied ice to the injured area.

"Back away," he told her again, this time with a shade less agony throbbing around the order.

Chapter Two

Okay, if he didn't want her to help him, then she was absolved of her guilt and free to go, MacKenzie thought. As soon as he did one little thing.

"Okay, I'll back away," MacKenzie said gamely to the man who was trying very hard not to double over, "as soon as you move your truck." She indicated the slightly dusty cherry-red car in the carport. She'd had it washed just last weekend, but New York dust was a tenacious thing to reckon with. "You're blocking my Mustang."

It took all of Quade's self-control not to growl at the woman. Pain was still shooting out to all parts of him, making him feel as vulnerable as a day-old kitten. He didn't particularly like that self-image. The little red-head had really swung that case of hers and hit him smack where he lived.

It took effort just to draw a breath. Quade bit down hard on the inside of his lower lip to keep from making any sounds that would give away the level of pain he was enduring. He had his hand clamped down onto the side of the truck to keep from falling to his knees, which were still trying to buckle.

"Right" was all he managed to get out.

Swallowing, he dug deep into his pocket for the keys. Somehow, he managed to get himself behind the wheel of the truck even though every movement brought its own penalty. Throwing the gearshift into Drive, he pulled the truck up several car lengths, allowing the woman to have access to her vehicle.

When he got out, his knees were only marginally in working order.

"Thank you," the redhead said over her shoulder as she bounced into her car.

He remained standing by the truck, waiting out the pain that was driving sharp carpenter's nails into his entire body.

As she pulled out, the woman offered him what he surmised was an apologetic smile. It didn't begin to cover her transgression. Because he didn't want to move just yet if he didn't have to, Quade followed with his eyes the red Mustang's progress as the woman drove out of the complex.

A plume of smoke was coming out of the vehicle's tailpipe. She was burning oil. It figured.

Quade sighed, straightening slowly. He had to get back to work. He had exactly one day—today—to settle in before he had to report for his new position at the

Wiley Memorial Research Labs. And begin his new life.

And hopefully find a way to move on.

It had not been a good day.

Twice, during the course of her workday, MacKenzie had found herself on the verge of breaking down. Both times Dakota had been near her. She'd almost told her best friend that she was pregnant.

But each time she'd begun, the words had stuck to the roof of her mouth, refusing to be dislodged. She'd shared absolutely everything with Dakota in the years that she'd known her and thought of the woman as almost a twin sister. But her pregnancy was something she needed to get used to herself before she could bring herself to talk to anyone else about it.

Hoping against irrational hope that this was all some rebellious act by her body, she'd decided to reschedule her exam with her doctor. She'd asked the nurse to try to squeeze her in somehow.

MacKenzie got lucky. There'd been a cancellation just called in. Consequently, Lisa, Dr. Neubert's nurse, put her down for one o'clock. With butterflies strapping themselves onto Boeing jets inside her stomach, she told Dakota that she was grabbing a late lunch and would be back in time for the show, then bolted.

Less than twenty minutes later, she found herself draped in tissue paper and lying on the examination table, counting holes in the ceiling tiles while Dr. Ann Neubert, her doctor for the last five years, performed an internal exam.

The second Dr. Neubert withdrew, MacKenzie propped herself up on her elbows and tried vainly to read the blond woman's expression.

"I'm wrong, right?" MacKenzie asked eagerly, praying for confirmation.

Ann had stripped off her gloves, throwing them into the small trash basket.

"No, you're right." The woman's expression was soft, encouraging, as if second-guessing her patient's anguish. "Babies bring rainbows into your life—a new way of seeing things."

Oh God, it's true. I'm really pregnant. Now what am I going to do?

She wasn't ready for this, not by a long shot. "Easy for you to say," MacKenzie had muttered audibly. "You have a husband."

Her doctor had surprised her then by putting down her chart and sitting down on the table beside her.

There was an earnest, faraway look in her eyes as she said, "I didn't when I first found out that I was pregnant." And then she laughed. "My first daughter was the result of an all-but-out-of-body, wild, impetuous experience one star-filled night on the beach with a handsome journalist who was going overseas to cover war stories the very next day."

MacKenzie vaguely remembered the woman had two beautiful little girls and an even more beautiful husband who earned his living writing for one of the larger newspapers. "Isn't your husband a journalist?"

Ann winked at her. "Turned out to be one and the same." The doctor took hold of her hands, which made her feel just for a moment a sense of calm, that things would work out. "What I'm saying is that perhaps you and the baby's father—"

And the calm vanished. She shook her head. "Not going to happen. He went back to a wife I didn't know he had."

MacKenzie sighed deeply. Everything always happened for a reason, her grandmother had been fond of saying. Maybe there was a reason behind this, too, although for the life of her, she didn't see one.

"Besides, looking back, maybe I didn't really love him in quite that 'forever' kind of way." Helpless to continue, she shrugged.

Ann laid a hand on her shoulder. "Things have a way of working out. You'll see. If not one way, then another." And then she paused just before leaving. Her eyes were drawn to the small oval at the hollow of MacKenzie's throat. "Nice cameo. New?"

MacKenzie fingered it. So far, it was turning out to be a dud. "Yes, it is. Thanks."

Ann nodded, then dug into one of the pockets of her lab coat. "If you need to talk, this is my private number." Ann pressed a card into her hand before leaving the room.

MacKenzie was off the table in a blink of an eye. There was a show to oversee.

She didn't remember the trip back. It was one huge blur, hidden behind the recurring mantra: *You're pregnant, you're pregnant.* Her head throbbed.

The call to Jeff was made the first chance she got, right after the program had wrapped for the day. Even as she tapped out the old, familiar number, she could feel the butterflies in her stomach going into high gear again. But it had to be done. There was no way around it. Jeff had a right to know. And she wanted to get this over with as fast as possible.

Jeff listened in silence as she choked out the words. When she finished, he was sympathetic and supportive, all the things that had attracted her to him in the first place.

And then he said, "Listen, Mac, if you need money to get this taken care of—"

"I don't," she said, cutting him off before he could say anything further.

"Then you're keeping it?" There was a clear note of surprise in his voice.

Of course she was keeping the baby, she thought indignantly. How could she not? She'd always had a fondness for all creatures smaller than she was. She just wasn't relishing the notion that her whole life would be replumbed and restructured.

Hormones mounting another rebellion in her system, MacKenzie didn't like the way he dehumanized what was happening. "It's a baby, Jeff, not an 'it.'"

There was another long pause, as if he were choosing his words carefully. "I'm not interested in being a father, Mac."

Something shut down in her. It wasn't that she was expecting him suddenly to declare that he'd been blind and could now see and from here on in everything was going to be coming up roses for them, but she didn't like the guarded way he was approaching this. As if she wanted something from him. As if he were bracing himself for some kind of shakedown.

Her voice grew more formal. "I know that. I just thought you had a right to know that there would be someone walking around with half your gene pool."

She swore she heard a sigh of relief. When Jeff uttered the next words, he sounded more like his old self. "I'll have my lawyer draw up papers making arrangements for child-support payments."

For some reason, that just made her angrier. "I didn't call you for that."

"I know. But I want to do this. I'll be in touch." He hung up as if afraid that she might still hit him up for something.

She let the receiver drop back into the cradle within the small cubbyhole that was her office. And then left it at that. Left it with a hollow feeling in the pit of her stomach right beside the seedling that was her baby.

Her baby, not his, not anyone else's. Hers, she thought with a sudden cloud of tears welling up within her eyes.

Grabbing a tissue, she blocked a wave of exasperation. There they went again, her emotions climbing onto the same roller coaster they'd been riding for the last week. Damn but she was going to have to get a handle on all this emotional stuff before she found herself being utterly derailed.

Somehow, she made it through the remainder of the day, avoiding Dakota's probing questions and getting everything prepared for the next day's taping. Instead of staying beyond six, the way she normally did, she made it out the first second she could.

Pausing only long enough to pick up the take-out food she'd ordered earlier, MacKenzie had every intention of going home and locking herself up in her apartment. She wanted to keep the world at bay for as long as she could. Heaven knew, this wasn't something that she could keep a secret indefinitely, although there had been women who had managed just that because of minimal weight gain and a bevy of very wide, very loose clothing.

She doubted she'd be that lucky.

The same truck was still there when she pulled into the parking lot behind her complex. But this time it wasn't blocking her space. The vehicle was stretched out over three empty spaces in guest parking. Some of the tenants with visitors weren't going to be happy tonight.

Not her concern, she thought, guiding her Mustang into her spot.

The take-out bag still felt mildly warm, which meant that the food within the cartons was at least equally so, if not more. The thought of warm food was oddly comforting.

Until it hit her mouth, she thought wryly. After that, all bets were off.

She picked up her purse and shifted the bag to her other side. Approaching her apartment, she saw that the door to the apartment beside hers was wide open. She recognized a piece of furniture from the truck and tensed.

This meant that the guy she'd all but robbed of his manhood was going to be her new neighbor. MacKenzie caught her lower lip between her teeth. Talk about making a bad first impression....

Pausing, she peered inside the apartment but 'didn't see him anywhere. She squelched the desire to go inside, not wanting him to add the word *trespasser* to his list of grievances against her. The living room was in a state of upheaval. There were boxes clustered everywhere. Had he been moving in all day? Of course he had. Most men were domestically challenged. Moving was a major event to them, right up there with wars and famine and flash floods.

MacKenzie knew she should be moving on before her mildly warm dinner became stone cold. But she'd been diagnosed as terminally curious as a child and couldn't quite get her feet to move away from the doorway.

Was there a Mrs. New Neighbor somewhere? The signs she saw said otherwise. The furniture seemed definitely masculine, but then some women favored clean, unobstructed lines and minimal furnishings.

He was nowhere in sight.

"Hello?" she called out. When there was no answer, she raised her voice and repeated the greeting.

This time, she got a response.

Quade came walking out from the rear of the apartment. The moment he saw her, a note of tension invaded his otherwise impassive expression. She was carrying something in a brown paper bag and her offending purse/weapon was suspended from her wrist. Quade watched it warily, then raised his eyes to her face.

"Should I be grabbing a tray or something to deflect any more blows?"

MacKenzie laughed and flashed him what she felt was her best smile, the one she knew took in her eyes, as well as her lips. "Sorry about this morning."

"Okay." He said the word as if it were meant to terminate any further conversation.

By all rights, this was her cue to withdraw. But she didn't like the idea of having someone living next door who bore a grudge against her. It didn't take much imagination to see that was what was in the works here. What was needed right now was a little damage control.

MacKenzie thought of the take-out bag tucked against her side.

Because he'd turned his back on her and had begun tearing the tape off a box that was almost as tall as she was, she took a step inside the apartment.

"Hungry?"

He didn't even spare her a look. "Why, you have some rat poison you want to unload?"

She could feel her back going up, but she forced her voice not to sound hostile as she asked, "Not very friendly, are you?"

This time, he did spare her a look. It was the kind of look that made men with black belts in karate take two giant steps backward. "In general I try to avoid people who try to castrate me."

She didn't own a black belt in karate, or any other color belt for that matter, but she had been raised with three brothers and had adopted feistiness as her middle name. "That was an accident."

"And you apologized." His tone was cold and gave

no indication of what he was thinking, other than the fact that he didn't want to be bothered right now and was dismissing her.

She dug in. "Yes, I did."

"Apology accepted." What did it take to get this woman out of his living room and his apartment? Did he have to physically carry her out? He went back to removing the tape from the box he had no intentions of unpacking today. "Mission accomplished."

Suppressing a sigh, MacKenzie began to leave, then abruptly stopped.

No, damn it, she wasn't going to add this to the list of things that bothered her. She was going to prove she was a friendly neighbor if she had to nail his hide to the closet door.

"After work I stopped at Sam Wong's."

He frowned as he looked at the contents within the box. It had been mislabeled. These things belonged in the kitchen. Okay, so maybe he would unpack a few things, he decided. "Good for you."

Since he'd left himself open for a moment, she jumped right in. "They have the best Chinese takeout in the city."

He began to drag the box into the kitchen, doing his best to ignore this woman who was bent on invading his apartment. It was akin to trying to ignore a jack-in-the-box that kept popping up at inopportune times. "I'll keep that in mind."

She followed him into the small kitchen. The management had just had it painted a stark white that was all but blinding. She squinted slightly to compensate. "I bought more than I could eat for dinner."

Digging into the box, Quade hauled out a stack of carefully wrapped dishes. His sister had packed them while trying to talk him out of moving. But it was something he had to do, at least for now. At least until the hole in his gut got smaller.

"Wasteful," he commented.

She was barely two steps away from exploding. Why was he treating her as if she were some kind of leper when all she was doing was trying to be neighborly? "Would you like to share some?"

Putting the wrapped dishes on the counter, he finally looked at her. "Why would you share it with me?"

"Maybe it's your sparkling personality I can't resist."

For a second, he looked as if he would chew her up and spit her out whole. But then he surprised her. He laughed. Just before he dug into the box again for a second stack of dishes. "Then I'd say you had a serious problem."

"I don't, but you might." The bag was beginning to get heavy. MacKenzie leaned it against the counter. "Are you always like this?"

He hadn't the vaguest idea what she was talking about. All he knew was that Carla had packed too many things. All he really needed was a single setting, not eight. That had been Ellen's domain. She was the one who'd liked company. All he'd ever liked was Ellen.

"Like what?" he bit off.

"Like you're Mr. Wilson and everyone else is Dennis the Menace."

He stopped unpacking and gave her a long, penetrating look that ended with a glance toward her purse. "Only when confronted with Dennis."

"Meaning me."

Polite lies had never been part of his makeup. "See anyone else around?"

The way she saw it, she could either turn on her heel, tell him to go to hell and retreat into her apartment, or start over. Because she was an optimist at heart and hated the thought of anyone disliking her, she opted to start over.

Leaving her purse on the counter, she put out her hand. "I think we got off to a wrong start. My name is MacKenzie Ryan."

He stood contemplating the extended hand for a moment, as if shaking it were a step he wasn't prepared to take, then shrugged before slipping his strong, bronzed fingers around hers.

"Quade Preston." He didn't bother giving her his job title. The less he shared, the better. Dropping her hand, he turned away. "Now if you'll excuse me, I have work to do."

Oh well, she'd tried.

"On that sparkling personality, no doubt." Turning on her heel, MacKenzie, her purse and her belated peace offering began to walk away.

She was almost at his door when she heard him say, "You need an oil change."

MacKenzie stopped and turned around. Part of her thought that she'd imagined hearing his voice. "Excuse me?"

"An oil change," Quade repeated. "Your car's burning oil." He shoved the half-emptied box aside. "Saw it as you pulled away this morning."

MacKenzie ventured back into the room. "You're a mechanic?"

He shook his head, walking out of the kitchen and past her. God, he was tall, she thought.

"Just observant. When was the last time you changed your oil?" His deep voice floated back to her out of the bedroom.

MacKenzie attempted to think. Car maintenance was one of those things that was strictly an afterthought with her. She knew that her father and brothers would have hooted about her negligence, but with everything she did, something had to go to the bottom of the list. In this case, it was the car.

"I remember that it was snowing."

"Might be easier if you went by the odometer instead," he told her, reemerging into the room. "Every three thousand miles is a good rule of thumb."

She pretended to examine her digit. "My thumb doesn't have any rules."

And neither, most likely, did she, he thought. No surprise there. "I had a feeling."

She decided to make another effort. "So, could I interest you in some Chinese?"

He'd grabbed a hamburger and fries at a fast-food restaurant when he'd gone to get gas for the truck, so hunger was not a problem at the moment. But the meal had come with a soft drink whose container could have been used to replenish a small lake. "I'd be more interested in your bathroom."

Her eyes narrowed. "Excuse me?" she said again.

He jerked his thumb toward the back, where his own bathroom was. "Super shut down the water coming into the apartment. Something about having to refit the pipe leading into the shower."

She drew the logical conclusion, picking up on the last thing he said. "So you can't take a shower."

"Or anything else."

She was very aware of the need for a bathroom. MacKenzie beckoned for him to follow her. "Sure. Come on in."

Walking out, she began to search through her purse for her keys. As she approached her own door, the take-out bag she was holding against herself was in danger of spilling its contents at her feet.

Seeing it tilt, Quade took the bag from her. She flashed him a smile as she dug farther into her purse.

He eyed the potential weapon with respect and disdain. "Just what do you keep in that thing?"

"My life," she replied.

He looked at the shape of the purse, which could have doubled as a portfolio case, something it once had been in her early days.

"Your life is large and flat?"

"Some days," she told him as she finally located her keys. Drawing them out, she hunted through the cluster for the right one.

He noted that there were at least fifteen keys on the ring. "Just how many doors do you need to unlock?"

"You'd be surprised." There was one for her apartment and one for her car. The other keys had to do with her place of work. "I'm an assistant producer." She gave him a sidelong glance as she zeroed in on the right key.

MacKenzie saw that he did not look impressed. But then, she was beginning to doubt that there was anything on the face of the earth that might actually impress the tall, dark, sexy and solemn male standing behind her.

Chapter Three

Finally finding the key for the front door, MacKenzie waited for Quade to politely ask exactly what she was the assistant producer of. But there was only silence at her back as she unlocked the door.

So she took the initiative. It wasn't exactly a stretch for her, given her natural exuberance and impatience. "It's for ...*And Now a Word from Dakota*."

Quade looked surprised by the piece of information she offered, as if it were a Frisbee that had come out of the blue and landed on his lap. "What is?"

Pulling her key out again, she opened the door. "The show where I'm the assistant producer."

He shook his head. "Sorry, never heard of it." And then, because he realized that probably sounded too abrupt, he added, "I'm not from around here."

Interest sparked her eyes as she dropped the key back into the cavernous regions of her purse. "Oh, where are you from?"

Quade looked around. Her apartment was a theme and variation of his, only in reverse. And with a smattering of feminine touches to it. "You ask a lot of questions."

"I don't when information's volunteered." She cocked her head, studying him. His expression was utterly impassive. What did he look like when he smiled? When he relaxed? *Could* he relax? He'd laughed earlier, but it had been too fleeting. By the time she'd looked at him, his smile—if it had ever appeared—had evaporated. "You're not the curious type, are you?"

"I'd say you've got enough for both of us in that category." Since MacKenzie looked as if she were waiting for some kind of a definite answer, he added, "But no, I'm not." No, he thought, that wasn't entirely accurate. "Not about people."

Her eyes narrowed as she tried to follow his thoughts. "What *are* you curious about?"

Quade generalized, not wanting to open the door to any specifics. He found it easier that way. "Diseases."

When he said that, she could envision him sitting in an easy chair, poring over textbooks with graphic photos. "That's a little morbid."

He'd never looked at it that way. To him it was his life's work. Therein lay the irony. "Not when it comes to saving lives."

Was he a doctor? Now that, she'd have less trouble believing. "Do you save lives?" she prodded when he said nothing.

He figured he'd been neighborly enough for one encounter. Hell, for all encounters until the end of the year. Maybe even beyond.

"Your bathroom?" he prompted, reminding her why he'd followed her into her apartment in the first place.

"Right through there." She pointed off to the rear of the nine-hundred-square-foot apartment. "Right by the master bedroom."

MacKenzie knew the term was a whimsical one inasmuch as it was the larger of the two bedrooms by perhaps a couple of square feet.

"Thanks," Quade murmured, quickly making his exit before she went off on another tangent that required some acknowledgment from him.

MacKenzie stood where she was for a moment. If her new neighbor wasn't so good-looking, he would have been a perfect blueprint for some kind of mad scientist. Withdrawn, uncommunicative. But he *was* good-looking and the sight of him brought posters for volleyball on the beach to mind. It wasn't a large stretch of the imagination for her to see lean muscles beneath his T-shirt. He probably had one of those abdomens where you could count the number of ridges that went into making up what someone had told her was called a washboard stomach.

The man would be like catnip to the women in the area, she thought.

You're swearing off everything male, from hamsters on up, remember? she reminded herself.

MacKenzie walked into her kitchen. With a shake of her head, she set down the take-out bag on the small table that was framed with four short, squat chairs.

There was no point in even thinking about him. Someone like the man presently using her bathroom undoubtedly had to be spoken for. Which was fine, because she wasn't in the market. And even if she were in the market, she was pregnant, so that pretty much put the lid on all things social.

Still, it didn't mean that she couldn't be friendly. She could always be friendly. MacKenzie sighed, unconsciously running her hand through her hair. She was counting on friends to take her mind off the chaotic turn of events in her life right now.

Feeling her appetite waning even though she still hadn't taken a bite of anything, MacKenzie took out a plate and utensils. Her hand hovered over the drawer as she wondered whether or not she should take out a setting for Quade, too.

He hadn't said anything about staying. But feeding him his first night here *would* be the neighborly thing to do. On a whim, she took out an extra fork and plate.

MacKenzie heard the bathroom door open just as she finished taking the cartons out of the now-damp paper bag. Bunching the bag up, she tossed it into the garbage pail and turned in time to see Quade walk by on his way toward the front door.

He wasn't staying, she thought and wondered where the wave of sadness came from. Was there something she could take to get her emotions to level off again?

Abandoning the kitchen, she crossed to the door. "You still didn't say where you were from."

He slid her a side glance. "No, I didn't."

"Why?" she prodded, "Is it a secret?"

Quade paused, thinking that perhaps he should have done a little research on his own rather than leaving the matter of finding him a place to live in the hands of a real-estate agency. Granted, this place was convenient, close to the laboratory and from the looks of it, rather a nice place to reside, as well.

But in truth, he didn't require very much anymore and this apartment definitely did have its detractions, he thought, looking at the exuberant redhead with the ever-moving mouth.

"Are all the neighbors like you?"

She wasn't sure exactly what he meant or how he meant it. "You mean inquisitive?"

Quade laughed shortly, although his lips never curved. "I was thinking of 'nosy,' but all right, we'll go with your word."

"Can't speak for everyone," MacKenzie allowed, "but the woman who lived here before you liked to take a healthy interest in what was going on and the people who came and went around here."

He read between the lines. "By 'healthy interest' you mean everything short of strapping someone to a lie-detector machine and assaulting him or her with a barrage of questions?"

She grinned at that image and he thought to himself that the expression added extra wattage to the room. "Something like that."

He supposed it wouldn't harm anything if he told her where he'd lived before everything inside of him had died. "I'm from Chicago."

She nodded, pleased by the step he'd taken. "I'm from Boston originally."

But he wasn't here to exchange information. He had no desire to get to know anything about any one of his neighbors, or the people he was going to be working with, for that matter. All he wanted to do was his work and wait for eventual oblivion, because that was what Ellen had left in her wake. A deep, vast hole that he found himself walking around in in slow motion.

The look in his eyes was meant to put the woman in her place. "I don't remember asking."

"No, I'm just volunteering." Her smiling eyes met his. "Anything else you want to know?"

Quade frowned. He was wasting time here. "I didn't even want to know that."

Her smile didn't wane. The man was clearly in need of someone to talk to before he became some kind of weird hermit. "Is that what's called being brutally frank?"

"That's what's called minding my own business." About to leave, he paused just for a moment. He had to ask. "I thought New Yorkers kept to themselves."

"That's just bad publicity by someone who never took the trouble to really get to know his neighbors." Delivering the salvo, she looked up at him and smiled brightly.

Ellen used to smile like that, Quade realized suddenly. Realized, too, that it had warmed him just to see it.

Abruptly, he straightened, as if being rigid could somehow keep the memories at bay. "I've got to get back to unpacking." He nodded toward the rear of the apartment. "Thanks for the use of the bathroom."

"Any time." She moved a little closer, matching him step for step. "Sure I can't interest you in an egg roll or something? They're small."

"No, thanks. I already ate," he told her. "I grabbed a burger and fries earlier."

"Then you didn't have dessert," she said suddenly. She switched positions quickly, swinging around to look at the contents she'd just removed from the bag. She scooped up the first fortune cookie she came to and offered it to him. "Here."

He was about to refuse, decided that it would just be wasting his breath, that he'd wind up with the cookie in some form or other no matter what he said. So he nodded instead and was immediately rewarded by having a fortune cookie thrust into his hand.

"Thanks."

He looked as if he were going to shove the cookie straight into his pocket without looking at it. Where it was probably going to stay until he sent the pants to the cleaners. If he bothered taking it out then, MacKenzie thought.

She caught his wrist before he could get his hand into his pocket. He looked at her in surprise. "Aren't you going to open it? I know you've got this 'no curiosity' thing going, but me, I've always love reading fortune cookies."

He was all set to give it back to her. "Then you keep it."

But she held up her hands, warding off the exchange. "No, bad luck to take a used fortune cookie. It's yours now."

He sighed, debating just leaving but he had a feeling she would pop up like toast in his place the next morning, asking what the fortune cookie had to "say." Since she wouldn't take it back, he was stuck.

Quade cracked open the cookie and pulled out the small white paper. "Destiny has entered your life," he read, then crumpled the paper.

No, it hadn't, he thought. Destiny had left his life. With the last breath that Ellen had taken. "Happy?" he asked.

"For now," she answered truthfully.

Well, at least she didn't try to lie. Quade nodded curtly at her as he walked out her door.

MacKenzie hurried after him, crossing the threshold. The sky looked as if it was going to rain at any moment. The air smelled pregnant with moisture. MacKenzie shook her head. She had pregnancy on the brain.

"Let me know if you need anything else," she called after him.

The only acknowledgment she received was another quick, dismissive nod before he closed the door behind himself. She heard the lock click into place.

"Good-looking fella."

Startled, MacKenzie bit back a squeal of surprise. She turned and saw that there was a short, slightly rounded older woman standing in the doorway of the apartment that was two doors away.

The woman had frosted hair cut short and looked to be somewhere in her late fifties, possibly early sixties. Her blue eyes were sparkling as they took in Quade. It seemed to MacKenzie that the woman was stroking the dog she was holding a tad too hard. The dog, a Jack Russell terrier, softly growled his displeasure until she finally stopped petting him.

Careful what you wish for, Dog, MacKenzie cautioned silently.

"New neighbor," MacKenzie volunteered out loud, nodding toward Quade's apartment.

Finding herself no longer hungry for food and in no mood for the solitude she'd told herself she'd been craving all afternoon, MacKenzie crossed to the older woman. The woman didn't look the slightest bit familiar. MacKenzie would have remembered someone who could have easily been cast in the role of Mrs. Claus.

"I'm sorry, did you just move in, too?"

"Me?" One hand went to her ample bosom as the woman laughed at the idea. The sound was rich, bawdy and not entirely in keeping with the angelic-looking rest of her. "No, Cyrus and I have been here for ages."

"Cyrus?"

"My dog."

"Oh." MacKenzie looked at the woman more closely. Nope, not familiar at all. "I'm sorry, I've got a very hectic, erratic schedule. I guess I just never bumped into you."

The woman's smile was almost cherubic. "No, you haven't. Can't say I wouldn't mind 'bumping' into that young man, though." The woman peered around MacKenzie, as if hoping to get another glimpse of Quade. But the door at his apartment remained closed. If he was going to be bringing up any more furniture or boxes, it wasn't now. "He's been moving in all day."

MacKenzie nodded. "Yes, I know."

Interest etched itself into the older woman's soft features. "Do you also know his name?"

"Quade Preston." MacKenzie liked the way that sounded. Strong.

The other woman seemed to be trying it out in her head, as well. She nodded at MacKenzie. "Very masculine sounding. Doesn't look very friendly, but maybe that's because he's new," she theorized. "Shy so often can come off as standoffish, don't you think?"

"Yes, I suppose so."

MacKenzie considered herself shy, but she took just the opposite tack, trying to force herself to be as friendly as possible. Obviously it wasn't working with her new neighbor.

As if someone had just snapped their fingers, the other woman seemed to come out of a self-imposed trance. She stopped looking toward the other apartment with a bemused expression on her face and faced MacKenzie instead.

"Oh, where are my manners?" The woman shifted the dog she was still holding to her other arm, putting out her hand toward MacKenzie. A thin layer of downy dog fur clung to her sleeve. "I'm Agnes Bankhead. Aggie to my friends." Her eyes brightened as MacKenzie took her hand. "And I think we're going to be friends—as long as you tell me your name."

MacKenzie took an instant liking to the older woman. There was something about Aggie that reminded her of an aunt she'd had. Actually, Sara had been her father's aunt, but so young at heart, she'd seemed years younger than her dad.

"MacKenzie."

Aggie cocked her head, the ends of her short silver-gray hair swinging about her face. "Is that first or last?"

"My mother's last, my first." She'd been named after her mother's people. She was also supposed to have been a boy. The name would have fit better. But when she was born, her mother had been adamant that the name be used. She hadn't intended on having any more children. Ethan, the brother who'd arrived eleven months after MacKenzie, had had other ideas. "It's MacKenzie Ryan."

Aggie firmly shook her hand before releasing it. "Well, MacKenzie Ryan, it's nice to finally meet you."

MacKenzie was still amazed that this was their first encounter. You would have thought, living so close together in the same small complex, that their paths would have crossed at least once before. "How long did you say you lived here?"

"You're wondering that because you never saw me before, right?" Aggie guessed knowingly. "There's a reason for that. I worked at home." She waved at hand toward her front door. "Glued to my computer, going blind. Until last week, my last job was freelance graphic artist." She leaned her head in closer, as if sharing a secret. "Freelance is shorthand for fighting to keep the wolf away from the door. Most of the time, the wolf won."

She stopped abruptly, looking up. The sky was a deep shade of gray layered over black. "Looks like more rain's about to find us. Why don't you come inside and I'll finish this conversation?"

MacKenzie was more than happy to take her up on the invitation.

"I'd love to." She followed Aggie and her dog into the cozy apartment. "So, what happened last week?"

Aggie closed the door and released the dog, who immediately trotted off to his favorite chair. A large dark blue recliner with an crocheted afghan spread over it.

"Last week I took a long, hard look at my life and realized that I was tired of hustling for clients. I decided that if I was going to hustle, I might as well do it for the kind of self-satisfaction that would make me feel loved."

MacKenzie caught her lower lip between her teeth, afraid to venture a guess about the new career the other woman had chosen for herself. For one thing, Aggie's choice of words sounded way too much like a description a former high-profile madam had given Dakota on one of the shows they'd done earlier this year.

Bright and vivacious, Aggie still looked a little old to be getting her feet wet in the game, although who knew? MacKenzie decided to play it safe and just ask.

"Such as?"

Aggie grinned from ear to ear, her expression catapulting her into her thirties, or thereabouts. "Stand-up comedy."

MacKenzie stared at her. It took years to become a successful comedian. Years of one-night stands and playing in clubs that had more roaches than customers seated at the tables. She couldn't have heard Aggie correctly. "Excuse me?"

The look in the sparkling blue eyes was knowing. And there was laughter in them, as well. "You think I'm out of my mind, don't you?"

The last thing MacKenzie wanted was to offend the woman. Besides, who was she to judge anything? She'd judged that Jeff was the perfect man and look how wrong that turned out to be?

"No, absolutely not. I think everyone should try to make their dreams come true."

"Just not at seventy-two."

"Seventy-two?" MacKenzie echoed incredulously. "You're seventy-two?" How could she have been that far off? Maybe being pregnant affected your vision, she thought.

"Uh-huh." With one hand at her back, Aggie gently guided her into her cheery kitchen. Daffodils bloomed on the wallpaper, adding to the feeling of warmth in the room. "I know, I know, I don't look a day over seventy-one. It's all those genes I inherited from my mother." Switching on the coffeemaker on the counter, Aggie poured in water and placed the pot under the spout. Hot water emerged almost immediately, making noise as it ran its course. "Of course, they're a little old themselves, having been used by her, not to mention all those women who came before her."

After turning around, she paused to lean against the counter. "They tell me that my great-great-great-grandmother looked like she was fifteen when she was my age, but what can you do?" Crossing to the small pantry, she opened the door and reached inside. "Tea?" she asked, firing the question over her shoulder.

Maybe Aggie had something there, MacKenzie thought. The woman was certainly entertaining and amusing. Maybe she was unique enough to make it in this unsteady field she was thinking of entering.

"Um, yes, please."

Taking out a small box of tea bags, Aggie placed the box on the counter in front of MacKenzie. The coffee-maker had finished turning cold water into hot. "Earl Grey, right?" Aggie took down a cup and saucer. "No milk."

It was exactly the way she took her tea. And she was a tea drinker in a land of coffee consumers. It wasn't often that she was offered her first choice right out of the box.

She looked at Aggie with no small amount of wonder. "How did you…?"

The water steamed as it descended over the tea bag. Aggie set down the pot and waited a moment, then raised and lowered the tea bag a total of five times before setting it before her guest.

"I'm just a wee bit psychic at times. That, too, came from my mother's side," she confided with pride. "She came to this country from Scotland as a young girl. A lot of people had the sight—that's what they called it back then."

"Of course they had no cable television, so I suppose they had to do something to entertain themselves," she added. MacKenzie hadn't begun to drink, so Aggie gestured toward the tea. "Drink it while it's hot, dear. The nice tea will help to soothe your stomach."

MacKenzie looked at her sharply. "What makes you say that?"

Aggie's expression was the personification of innocence. "The baby's been giving you trouble, hasn't it, dear?"

MacKenzie's mouth dropped open.

Chapter Four

"How did you—" Realizing that her question was an admission, MacKenzie gathered her wits about her and started over again. "I mean, why would you think I was pregnant?"

When she made no move to pick it up, Aggie urged the warm teacup into her hands. "You have that look about you. I can more or less look into a woman's eyes and know if she's in the family way or not. Saw more than my share when I was midwifing." She smiled in response to the uncertain expression on MacKenzie's face. "I wasn't always a graphic artist. That's coming back in style, you know, being a midwife." And then she added with a measure of certainty, "Don't worry, I won't tell anyone. Not their business.

"Mine, neither," Aggie continued, "except that I've

always been the type who liked to know things about pretty much everyone I come in contact with." Aggie lowered herself into the chair on the opposite side of the oval kitchen table. Shifting, she made herself comfortable. "Guess you could call me a people junkie." Her smile widened. "Pick up a lot of things that way, too." Leaning forward, Aggie looked at her pointedly. "Like did you know that a little bit of ginger in your food helps with morning sickness?"

This was news to her. But then, so was the pregnancy. "Ginger? Like in ginger ale?" She'd heard that seltzer water and crackers helped some women. All it did for her was make matters that much worse.

"No, like in the spice." Aggie got up and went to the pantry, retrieving a small metal container. She placed it on the table beside the teacup. "Sprinkle it on things. It'll help settle your stomach." The smile on Aggie's lips was motherly as her eyes swept over her guest. "This'll all be behind you soon enough."

"Or in front," MacKenzie quipped, looking down at her very flat belly and picturing it distended and rounded out with a baby. She'd never thought much about having a family, but now the matter had been decided for her.

Aggie nodded at her with approval. "Sense of humor even under the gun. I like that." Reaching over the table, she patted MacKenzie's hand. "You'll survive well, MacKenzie. A sense of humor is what sees us through the worst of times."

MacKenzie didn't feel all that humorous right now. Thinking about the future made her feel as if she were staring into a deep, dark abyss. "Is that why you want to become a stand-up comedian?"

Aggie's eyes sparkled again, as if they were hiding a joke all their own. "That, and because I'm funny. Or so people have told me. And it's something new," she philosophized, "I like trying new things and new jobs. Keeps you young."

MacKenzie liked having things certain, liked knowing what tomorrow was going to bring. The unknown obviously didn't bother Aggie. Part of MacKenzie wished she could be that adventurous. "Well, something must be working because you really don't look your age. I thought you were in your fifties."

The compliment brought a genial smile to Aggie's lips. "I've got a feeling we're going to be very close friends, girl." Aggie nodded at the cup that was still sitting in its saucer. "Now drink your tea while it's hot."

"Yes, ma'am." Picking up her cup, MacKenzie brought it to her lips and drank.

MacKenzie stayed at Aggie's a great deal longer than she'd thought she would when she'd first crossed the threshold. By the time MacKenzie returned to her apartment, the dinner she'd brought home with her had become stone cold. What there'd been of her appetite had gotten appeased at the other woman's table. Aggie had given her a small portion of chicken à la king served over steaming rice. Oddly enough, it had been MacKenzie's favorite thing to eat as a child and she'd said as much to Aggie, who merely smiled at the information.

The older woman had sprinkled some ginger over the

serving, mixing it in before placing the plate before her. Aggie had winked and promised that MacKenzie would be a new woman by morning.

MacKenzie had had her doubts, but had eaten the meal with surprising relish.

Finally home in her own apartment, she gathered up the containers of Chinese food and stored them in her refrigerator. After wiping off the tabletop, she went to bed.

Accustomed to tossing and turning, she dropped off immediately.

It was the doorbell that woke MacKenzie, slicing through dreams until it took on shape and form.

Reluctantly opening her eyes, MacKenzie automatically turned toward the clock on the nightstand. As she did, the thought hit her that she'd forgotten to set her alarm. The doorbell had woken her half an hour before she was due to get up.

She wasn't sure if that was fortunate or not.

She struggled to rouse herself. Who could be at her door at this hour?

Jeff with a change of heart?

MacKenzie bolted upright, throwing the twisted covers off and hurrying into the matching half robe that had been haphazardly thrown on the edge of the covers. Abandoning the slippers that stood waiting for her feet at the foot of the bed, she groggily stumbled her way to the front door.

"You came," she cried even before she'd finished swinging it open.

The next second, disappointment drenched her.

Waking from a deep sleep had left the remnants of a dream still hovering in her brain. On the other side of her threshold stood a half-naked Quade. Swallowing, she glued her tongue to the roof of her mouth.

She'd been right about his abdomen. He did have a washboard stomach. As a matter of fact, he had the kind of stomach that caused washboard manufacturers—if there was such a thing anymore—to flock to his doorstep just for a knee-disintegrating look. A pair of frayed, cutoff jeans were hanging on for dear life along hips that were taut and slim. The very sight of which would have sent scores of men rushing to their local gyms, entertaining wild delusions of imitation.

He looked a little taken aback by her greeting. "Yeah, I did," he acknowledged, his expression all but saying that he wondered why she sounded so excited by his appearance on her doorstep. "There's still no running water," he told her in a tone that seemed the closest thing to an apology he'd ever get.

Blinking, she realized that Quade was carrying a large towel besides the small toiletry kit that undoubtedly housed soap and shaving paraphernalia. There was the makings of a seven o'clock shadow on his face, and he was a man in search of a bathroom to make his own.

Quade nodded toward the rear of the apartment. "I was wondering…"

He looked really uncomfortable, she realized. MacKenzie had a feeling that it had taken a great deal for him to approach her. It took no great student of human nature to guess that he wasn't the kind who liked asking for favors. Probably because he didn't like being in anyone's debt, no matter how trivial it was.

MacKenzie stepped back, opening the door wider. "Sure. Come on in."

He crossed the threshold, then looked back at her. She was trying to hide the disappointment skewering through her. "You weren't expecting me, were you?"

She pressed her lips together, debating lying, then shook her head. "No."

"Then that greeting—"

She cut him off before he could ask any questions. She wanted the matter closed. "Was for someone else." To her surprise, she saw what looked like a smattering of a smile curving his mouth. She was tempted to touch it, just to see if she wasn't hallucinating and that he was actually standing there. She kept her hands at her sides. "What?"

His smile was soft, sexy. "Looks like I'm not the only one who can be closemouthed if the situation calls for it."

Quade watched her pull together the ends of her robe. Not that the movement did anything to hide the body beneath. The material was close to translucent, covering a sexy, abbreviated nightgown made of material that almost matched the outer cover. Both stopped tantalizingly across her upper thighs.

For a short woman, she gave the illusion of having long legs. Long, shapely legs that invited the eye to travel farther and the mind to fantasize.

Neither of which he had time for, Quade reminded himself. There was a new frontier to cross and the threads, such as they were, of a life to finally begin to pick up. "I'm not stopping you from taking your shower, am I?"

She glanced at the clock in the kitchen. "I'm not due to get up for about another fifteen minutes," she assured him.

He received the message loud and clear. "Sorry, I didn't mean to wake you."

She was finally coming around. It was hard standing so close to him and his naked chest and not being acutely aware of all her senses, even the ones that had been dormant. "You didn't. I had to get up to answer the door anyway."

Quade paused, frowning, playing the line over in his mind. "That makes no sense."

She shrugged and the robe slipped off her shoulder, along with the strap of the nightgown. She tugged both up again.

"Sounded better in my head," she confessed. "You take your shower. I'll make coffee for you."

As he began to leave again, her phrasing caught his attention. "You don't drink coffee?"

"Tea," she told him.

He didn't want her putting herself out for him. Didn't want that kind of give-and-take relationship between them. It was bad enough that he was forced to use her bathroom.

"Then don't bother yourself with the coffee. I'm in a hurry anyway. I like giving myself a lot of time when I'm heading somewhere new."

"Starting a new job?" she guessed.

He had no time to withstand the onslaught of questions he knew was coming, even if he had no one to blame but himself for opening up the floodgates.

Quade tossed a "Yes" in his wake as he hurried off to make use of her bathroom.

She tried not to notice just how low slung the waistband of his cutoffs actually was and that it threatened to slip down even farther with each movement.

She was so busy trying not to notice, it took her a few minutes to realize that her first stop this morning hadn't been to commune with the porcelain bowl and that her stomach was not lodged in her throat first thing, the way it had been for the last couple of weeks.

The lack of nausea hadn't registered itself with her brain until after she'd taken out the box of tea bags for herself.

She stopped, stunned. Waiting for a delayed wave. It didn't come.

"Son of a gun, it really does work," she muttered, pleased. The ginger actually worked. Aggie had been right, bless her.

MacKenzie smiled as she took in a deep breath and held it for a moment before releasing it again. It was nice to be able to greet the morning feeling like a human being again instead of something even the cat wouldn't drag in.

"Thanks again."

The deep baritone voice seeped into her consciousness a beat after the words were uttered. MacKenzie turned around from the stove where she was preparing breakfast, a real breakfast for a change. French toast with a dusting of confectioners' sugar.

Quade was standing a few feet away from her, poised to leave. Droplets of water were still evident in his hair and a few were on his chest, bearing silent testimony to the shower he'd just taken. She noted with just the smallest pang that the sexy stubble was gone, but he still wore the cutoffs. The damp towel was slung over his bare shoulder and he had something bunched up in his hand.

Underwear?

Did that mean he was going commando beneath those threadbare shorts of his? Her breath abruptly halted its journey through her lungs.

MacKenzie struggled to keep her mind from going there, but it was too late. She was experiencing a definite reaction around her stomach akin to a cross between an earthquake and a tidal wave.

Delayed morning sickness?

No, this felt more like something was flip-flopping at the pit of her stomach. Probably terrifying the baby, she thought.

It took her a second, maybe two, but she finally found her tongue. MacKenzie did her best to force an easy smile to her lips. "Look, why don't you stay for breakfast?" She saw the protest rising to his lips and beat him to it using logic. She figured he might like that. "Anything you use to cook your own, you won't be able to wash and there's no water to use for your coffee."

Quade quietly and neatly shot her reasons down one by one, telling himself it had been a mistake to come here. He had done it with great reluctance, but he couldn't very well show up his first day on the job looking like a hermit who had come out of hiding, even if that was the way he felt inside. And if he was going to use her water to shave, he might as well use it to shower, as well, and try to feel a little more human about the experience that lay ahead of him.

But he drew the line at anything more. "I don't really eat breakfast and from what I can see, there's a Starbucks or something similar located practically every twenty feet in this city."

MacKenzie looked at him, unfazed. She was not one to give up easily. Living with three brothers had taught her that.

"Difference is, I won't charge you three dollars and change for a cup," she told him, already filling the one she'd taken out for him. She pushed the cup and saucer along the counter, moving it right in front of him. "You take it black, don't you?"

Well, since it was there, staring him in the face, he might as well drink it. He didn't believe in wasting things. "How did you know?"

She smiled, putting a tea bag into the cup of hot water she'd already poured. "You look like the black-coffee type."

"Black like my soul?"

Quade had no idea where the words had come from, only that, once spoken, they mirrored what he was feeling. Like his soul was this deep, black hole. Just as it had been before his late wife, Ellen, had come into it.

"I wasn't going to go that far," she told him.

Taking the French toast out of the pan and sliding it onto a plate, she sprinkled a tablespoon of confectioners' sugar over the thick slice. She placed the plate next to his coffee, along with a container of maple syrup with a dancing bee on the label. "So, where's this new job you're starting today?"

Normally, he didn't eat breakfast, just as he'd told her. But the French toast did look good. More than that, it smelled good. Almost as good as she did. Picking up a fork, he sank it into the toast, preferring not to drench the offering in syrup but to enjoy the light sugar taste unobstructed.

"Is that the rate of exchange?" he asked.

She had no idea what he was talking about. "Excuse me?"

"You said you wouldn't charge me three dollars for coffee," he reminded her. "I just want to know if questions are what you settled on in exchange for breakfast."

Taking his first bite, he found that the offering nearly melted on his tongue. And that he was hungry despite what he'd thought.

"Not questions," MacKenzie corrected smoothly with a soft smile as she made eye contact with him. "Answers."

He raised one muscular shoulder and let it drop again. She watched in rapt fascination. Up to this point, she'd thought that men who had builds like that were digitally enhanced as they made their way across the entertainment screen.

"My mistake."

"You haven't answered me."

Quade raised his eyes, if not his head. "No, I haven't."

After bringing over her tea, MacKenzie sat down on the stool beside his. The breakfast bar was what had been the deciding factor when she'd rented the apartment. She'd fallen in love with it. The bar and the fact that the apartments in the complex all formed an oval, overlooking a very small, very Spanish-looking courtyard. It gave the complex a communal feeling while existing in the middle of a bustling city that reportedly never slept and wasn't always known as the friendliest of places to an outsider.

The man was nothing if not evasive, she thought. Despite her leading questions, she hadn't gotten much information out of him. Normally by now, people had given her their life stories. She drew the only conclusion she could from the facts before her.

"Are you a spy?"

Quade nearly choked on his coffee, managing to swallow at the last minute and not embarrass himself. Her query brought to mind tall, darkly handsome men who were deadly with their hands and attracted impossibly gorgeous women. The image was so far from who and what he was.

"What?"

"A spy," she repeated. "One of those people sworn to chew a cyanide tablet rather than divulge what they were working on."

She looked normal enough, he thought, but then she'd said that she was an assistant producer and these entertainment types were usually two or three sandwiches shy of a picnic basket.

He wiped his lips with a napkin. "And, if I'm to follow this analogy, you're trying to get me to chew on a tablet?"

How had he leaped from point A to point B? "I'm

not asking you what you're working on, Quade." Even his name had spy possibilities, she thought. "Just a general 'where.'"

Eyeing her, he took a quick sip of coffee, then set down the cup before returning to the disappearing French toast. "In general, I'm working in New York."

She laughed, shaking her head. Maybe she *had* been right about him. He was certainly slippery enough to be a spy. "A little less general than that."

He'd made use of her shower and she was feeding him, not that he'd asked for the latter. But he supposed he owed her something. Besides, it was no secret what he was doing. It was just that he was an exceptionally private man. More so now that Ellen was gone. "I'm a research physician at Wiley Memorial Research Laboratories."

She stared at him in disbelief. "You're a doctor?" She'd never seen a doctor who looked like that. Her guess would have been physical-fitness trainer. Or spy, she thought with a grin.

"Research physician," Quade repeated. "I never practiced."

"You wouldn't have to." She set down her empty cup. "You look like the type who'd get it right the first time."

God, she was flirting, she realized suddenly. In her nightgown. Never mind that it was covered with an apron, she was still wearing a nightgown. What was wrong with her?

Abruptly, MacKenzie slid off the stool, making sure to hang onto the hem of her robe as she disembarked.

"Um, I've got to go get ready before I'm late for the studio," she murmured, avoiding his eyes. "Let yourself out when you're finished."

"Don't forget that oil change," he reminded her.

"Oil change?" she repeated the words dumbly. Her mind kicked in a beat later, remembering what he'd said about her car burning oil. "Oh, yeah, right. Will do."

With that, MacKenzie hurried back to her bedroom.

Shutting the door, she flipped the lock as an afterthought. She forced herself to focus on getting through her daily morning routine and not on the fact that there was a bare-chested, gorgeous, if uncommunicative, man sitting at her kitchen counter. Chewing.

It wasn't easy.

Chapter Five

Organized chaos, that was the only way she could view it. Her workday was complete organized chaos.

Which was all right with MacKenzie because at least it managed temporarily to get her mind off both her newfound delicate condition and the bare-chested man next door who had been gone by the time she'd gotten out of her shower. Gone from view, but not from mind. The traffic-filled trip to the studio had been filled with thoughts of him.

That had ended the moment she'd walked onto the set where the show was filmed each day. Nora Nigel was always early on the days she was featured on the show. Nora was an extremely personable animal trainer who always brought in strange, exotic animals to the show. A great crowd pleaser. Dakota had the woman and her ever-changing menagerie on every three to four months.

This time, among three other animals, Nora had brought a Peruvian snake with her. The snake, it seemed, had decided that today might be a perfect time to make a break for it and go exploring. Somehow, it had gotten out of its cage and was on the loose.

The members of the crew who had not been reduced to a quaking mass of panic were busy trying to locate the renegade reptile.

"Did I ever tell you I hated snakes?" MacKenzie asked Dakota as she walked into the latter's dressing room. After crossing the threshold, she carefully closed the door behind her, sealing them in. Hopefully sealing out the snake.

Having been part of the search for an hour, Dakota had finally retreated to her dressing room to go over her notes for the show.

She looked up from her pad. "I think you mentioned that very fact once or twice." Her expression was guardedly hopeful. "No news yet?"

MacKenzie's eyes swept around the room slowly. Part of her was waiting for the snake to come slithering out from some corner, ready to slide up to her neck and give new meaning to the word *choker.*

"From the snake, no. From the crew, the ones who haven't suffered a nervous breakdown are planning to conduct a mutiny if that thing isn't found quickly and caged." Fairly satisfied that the room was snake-free, she pulled up a chair and sat down beside Dakota. "I don't have to tell you that if that wretched snake isn't found by showtime, there isn't going to be a show. We'll have to put a rerun on in its place." She saw the protest rising to Dakota's lips and headed it off at the pass. "We can't have an audience in here with that snake running around loose—"

Humor played along Dakota's mouth. "Snakes can't run. They don't have feet."

"But they can make people sue the pants off us for gross mental anguish or whatever the popular term is for the current get-rich scenarios." She shook her head. "A snake, Dakota. Damn it, I should have said no."

"It's harmless," Dakota told her not for the first time.

MacKenzie shivered. To her, the only harmless snake was one that had been pronounced dead. Preferably a decade or more ago.

"It's really very tame," Dakota insisted. "Nora brought it in to show me earlier. I held it and it feels silky. You should try holding it when we get it back."

MacKenzie frowned. "I don't want to build a relationship with it. I just want it back where it belongs, in its cage."

Hearing the rise in her voice, Dakota held up her hand. "I know, I know. We'll find it before the show. Nora's very good about things like that."

MacKenzie thought she felt something against her leg and almost jumped six inches off her chair. But it was just her imagination. Slowly, she reseated herself. "What, finding snakes before people have heart attacks? She'd better hurry up."

Dakota laughed. It was obvious that MacKenzie was not about to be convinced. As a peace offering for whatever slight she might have given her assistant producer,

Dakota picked up the untouched half of her pastrami sandwich. "Want some?"

The moment she looked at it, MacKenzie felt her stomach come up into her throat like some animal that had crawled into a small space to die. Obviously ginger had a limited life expectancy, at least when it came to deactivating her nausea gland.

She tried to keep her stomach and its morning contents of French toast down. "No, thanks."

Dakota frowned, taking a closer look at her. "I've never known you to turn down pastrami, Zee. It's your favorite." She tried again. "C'mon, you can't be that nervous about the snake."

"I'm not," she told her flatly, avoiding Dakota's eyes. "I just don't want pastrami right now." Which was true. She didn't want anything right now, not after the deli meat's strong aroma was causing turmoil in her less-than-tranquil stomach.

"Zee, you're turning green." Dakota quickly placed the sandwich half back down on the waxed paper, concerned. "MacKenzie?"

MacKenzie wished Dakota would just drop it. "I said I'll be all right."

"Are you coming down with something?" Before MacKenzie could wave her away, Dakota leaned over and was feeling her forehead for signs of a fever.

She felt feverish, all right, but as for coming down with something, the only thing she seemed to be coming down with was terminal deception by continuing to be evasive with her best friend.

"Yes." And then she relented. She'd always hated

lies. "No." But she knew that opened her up to a world of questions. Frowning, she changed her story again to "Maybe."

"Well, that certainly explains everything." Dakota's eyes narrowed. And then she smiled broadly as a thought dawned on her. "You met someone, didn't you? See, I told you that the cameo—"

MacKenzie was quick to cut in before Dakota could get carried away. "Is a very nice, inanimate object that has absolutely no magical powers, Dakota. Which is just as well. Because the last thing I want to do is meet someone right now."

Dakota took a deep breath. "I know you're hurting over Jeff—"

"I am *not* hurting over Jeff." She turned away. "As it turns out, I think I really am better off without him."

Dakota's eyes kept widening, as if she were a volcano about to burst. Her fingers beneath MacKenzie's chin, she turned the woman's face toward her. And froze.

"Omigod. You're pregnant." The thought hit Dakota like a huge pile of bricks.

More than anything, MacKenzie wanted to deny it, to tell Dakota that she was being absurd. But avoiding the truth was one thing; lying was another. She'd never lied to Dakota.

Never lied very much, period. And besides, the evidence backing up her best friend's guess would be forthcoming soon enough. How would she feel about facing Dakota then?

Like an unexpected explosion that came without warning, exasperation filled her. MacKenzie slid off the chair and began pacing about the room. Warily, because she was still on the lookout for the wayward snake. "What, is it written on my forehead?"

"No, but sweat is," Dakota said softly, her heart going out to MacKenzie. "And green's a good color for you, unless it involves your skin." Dakota sighed, shaking her head, a million questions forming in her brain. "How? Who?"

What was the use in talking about it? It wouldn't change the end result. "I think you know the answer to both those questions, especially the first one." This sigh was deeper than the last. "Unless you skipped basic biology in middle school." She paused, then finally added, "Did you know that birth control is not a hundred percent guaranteed?"

Dakota reined in her pity, knowing that MacKenzie would only balk at it. As would she if the tables were turned. "Jeff?"

"Jeff," MacKenzie echoed.

Dakota pressed her lips together, knowing she had to tread lightly. "Have you told him?"

Unwilling to see anything remotely resembling pity in her best friend's eyes, MacKenzie deliberately looked away. "Yes."

"And?"

She barely raised a shoulder in a halfhearted shrug. "And he's offered to be financially responsible for the baby."

"How romantic." The sarcastic words burned on Dakota's tongue. She had never really cared for the man, but had done her best to be nice to him for

MacKenzie's sake. Now she would have liked to see him on the end of a barbecue skewer. "What a guy." She raised her eyes to MacKenzie's face. "I could ask Ian if he knows a hit man."

MacKenzie waved away the suggestion. When it came to Jeff, she'd already moved on.

Or so she had told herself.

"The man's gone back to his wife. And it wouldn't have worked out between us." She looked up to keep the tears from spilling out. Damn, but she hated being this emotional. "Besides, his ears were too big," she deadpanned.

"Definitely reasons for disqualification." Rising out of her chair, Dakota put her arm around MacKenzie's shoulders in a show of union and empathy. "Is there anything I can do?"

"You're doing it," MacKenzie told her quietly.

Dakota hugged her harder, wishing she could make everything right. "Anything. Anything at all. You name it."

MacKenzie nodded. Taking a deep breath, she got herself under control. "I guess you'll want the cameo back." She began to undo the ribbon, but Dakota stopped her.

"I've got my man. I can't use it. The rules say so." Dakota smiled brightly at her. "You hang on to it. You never know." A thought came to her. "Maybe the doctor who delivers your baby—"

MacKenzie knew exactly where Dakota was going with this. "It's a woman. And she's married," she added for good measure. She sighed haplessly. "Doesn't your plane ever land?"

Dakota slipped her arm from MacKenzie's shoulders. "I could remember a time when yours didn't."

"That was before I took on extra luggage."

Dakota kissed the top of her head, giving her a quick, warm squeeze. "We'll get through this," she promised softly.

MacKenzie was grateful for the unquestioning show of support. It helped her rally. Wiping away one stubborn, wayward tear with the back of her hand, she straightened and began to cross to the door.

"I'd better get back to the reptile search before the show's called off on account of snake."

With that, she left the room before Dakota had a chance to say anything else to her. Right now, MacKenzie was feeling very, very fragile. Damn those stupid hormones anyway.

She was going to get through this, MacKenzie told herself, just as Dakota had said.

She had no choice.

They finally found the snake. The reptile was curled up in Dakota's chair on the set. Nora quickly returned the offending snake to its cage just in time for the show. Things went more smoothly after that, but there were still a thousand details to see to before the tape was wound up and then another thousand details to address regarding the next day's show.

It felt like forever before MacKenzie could finally go home.

She was definitely dragging by the time she got into her Mustang. The only bright spot was that one of the staff gofers had gotten her car an oil change. At least she didn't have to worry about suddenly breaking down before she got to her complex the way Quade's expression seemed to prophesy that she would.

As she pulled into her parking spot that evening, MacKenzie felt as if all the energy had been siphoned out of her body. She'd turned down Dakota's invitation to join her and her brand-new husband for dinner. She didn't much feel like company.

Until she saw the car parked next to hers.

She didn't recognize the vehicle, but it was in the space assigned to the apartment next to hers.

Which meant it belonged to Bare-chested Man, she thought.

MacKenzie glanced at her watch. It was just before seven. Her new neighbor had reminded her of the type who left early for work and stayed late.

Wrong again.

"Batting zero, aren't you, Zee?" she murmured to herself as she got out of her car. She certainly hadn't been able to read Jeff well, had she?

With a sigh, feeling as if she weighed a thousand pounds instead of someone who had actually lost three pounds since the onset of her pregnancy, MacKenzie shrugged to herself. These things happened. If she were being utterly honest, things between her and Jeff probably wouldn't have worked out. She'd sensed that even before he'd sprung the news about his reconciliation with his wife on her.

There'd just been something missing in their relationship, that x factor she knew was necessary. The one that kept turning your knees into Jell-O even beyond the first few dates. The kind of feeling that Dakota had confided to her she had whenever she saw Ian.

That was what she wanted.

"Good luck," MacKenzie muttered under her breath. Oh, she fell "in love" fast enough, but she never stayed there emotionally after the initial shine began to wear off.

Which meant that she was probably going to die alone.

No, a small voice inside of her contradicted. *Not alone. You have a baby.*

Oh God, how was she ever going to be a mother?

As she approached her apartment, she saw that there was something taped to the door. To make the day perfect, that would have to be an eviction notice. Or a raise in rent.

God, when had she become this pessimistic?

Coming closer, MacKenzie found that it wasn't a notice from the housing development taped to her door— it was an invitation for dinner. From Aggie and Cyrus.

She removed the invitation from her door and smiled to herself. Maybe that was exactly what she needed, not solitude but a friendly stranger. She'd come close to breaking down twice at the studio today. Each time had had something to do with what Dakota had said. The woman's kindness undid her.

She needed to spend an hour or two in the company of a woman who was trying to perfect her comedy routine, MacKenzie thought. It was as good a diversion as any.

Slipping into her apartment, MacKenzie remained only long enough to freshen up.

When she walked by the kitchen on her way out again, she noticed that there were no dishes in the sink. She always left hers sitting there, too much in a hurry to get to them until later in the evening when she returned home again.

Belatedly, she remembered that when she'd come out of the shower this morning, Quade had already gone, but he'd left nothing in his wake. No dirty dishes, no coffee cup, nothing. Obviously he'd even washed out hers.

The man was incredibly neat. A rare thing these days, she mused.

After shutting and locking the door behind her, wishing she had something to bring besides her less-than-healthy appetite, MacKenzie made her way to Aggie's door.

An instrumental chorus of "Hello, Dolly" greeted her as she pressed the doorbell. It brought a smile to her lips. She loved musicals and went to the theater every chance she got.

The next moment, the door was opening and wonderful smells emerged, surrounding the cherubic-looking woman standing in the doorway.

Aggie seemed delighted to see her. "Ah, you got my note." Looking over her shoulder, she called out, "You can take the bread out of the oven. We can get started now."

Instantly MacKenzie hung back. This changed things. "You have company?"

Aggie looked directly into her eyes. MacKenzie could feel the touch of amusement in them. "I'd rather think of you as a friend-in-progress."

"No, I mean whoever you were just talking to just now—"

But as MacKenzie began to back away, Aggie took hold of her wrist, drawing her into the apartment. "Just another friend-in-progress," she informed her. "And also another potential place holder."

MacKenzie's brain felt fuzzy. "Place holder?"

"In my audience," Aggie told her, ushering her into the apartment. With a flip of her wrist, Aggie locked the door solidly behind her. She ushered MacKenzie into the tiny dining area. "Did I tell you I was going to be on at the Laugh-Inn? I need a few friendly faces in the audience to look at and Quade here half promised to be there." She patted MacKenzie's shoulder. "I was hoping you could work on him for me while I got the salad ready."

Just as Aggie mentioned his name, Quade moved into MacKenzie's line of vision.

To say that she was surprised to see him was an understatement comparable to saying that Noah and his family had taken a couple of pets on a cruise.

"What are you doing here?" The question slipped out before MacKenzie had a chance to stop it.

"Same as you, dear," Aggie said, cutting in. "Everyone's got to eat and not too many of you know how to cook these days. Fortunately, it's one of the things I'm quite good at. Besides, it's hard to say no to me." She winked, then waved her hands at both of them. "You two mingle while I get dinner on the table."

When MacKenzie made no effort to move from where she was standing, Aggie shooed her toward Quade.

MacKenzie shook her head, a fondness entering her heart despite the awkward situation. She'd never had a grandmother, but if she'd been able to put an order in, the woman would have been very much like Aggie. And Aggie was right. It was hard to say no to her. MacKenzie certainly couldn't. And that Aggie had managed to get Quade here was a testimony to exactly how persuasive the woman could be.

MacKenzie smiled at Quade, who looked a little disgruntled over being there. But that didn't change the fact that he was there. She didn't notice any indications on his wrists that he'd been bound and dragged over.

"She's something else, isn't she?" MacKenzie commented.

Quade took a sip from the glass of wine that Aggie had given him earlier. Normally, he didn't drink anything in the evening; he'd done enough of that as a teenager, losing himself in the wildness of youth. But Ellen had changed all that. For a while. When she'd died, he'd almost crawled into a bottle.

Eventually realizing Ellen wouldn't have wanted to see him that way had been what had made him crawl back out again and become all but a teetotaler.

But this was the first day of his new job and it was a social occasion, so he supposed that it was all right, as long as he kept it down to one drink. "That's one way to put it."

He didn't exactly sound thrilled to be here, but that didn't change the fact that he was still here. MacKenzie had a feeling that no one made Quade Preston do anything he didn't want to. Aggie had her vote for negotiator of the year.

She shook her head at the wine as he offered to pour her a glass. Instead, MacKenzie picked up the bottled water that was set out for them. "So, how did your first day go?"

He shrugged carelessly. His memory was a blur of names and faces. What remained clear in his mind was that the laboratory itself had been state of the art. And that was all that mattered. "All right."

"That's it?" Disappointment registered. She would have thought that the man would have been vocal about his work, if nothing else. "You can elaborate a little, can't you? You're not being judged on brevity here."

Taking another sip, he looked at her over the rim of his glass. "I wasn't aware I was being judged at all."

She shrugged casually, wondering what made the man tick. "Figure of speech."

Aggie stuck her head in from the kitchen and looked pointedly at Quade. "You need to loosen up, dear." The next moment, she emerged carrying a large salad bowl. He took it from her, earning a smile. "Right in the middle of the table will be fine." When he did as she asked, Aggie looked at him meaningfully. "But you still need to loosen up."

"My line of work doesn't exactly promote laughter."

"No, but it does promote hope," MacKenzie pointed out. It earned her a dark look. "You're looking for a way to find a cure for something, right? That means you're looking for a way to find hope for all these terminal people. A way to bring them laughter."

"Life," he corrected. "Not laughter."

"Life without laughter isn't worth living," MacKenzie told him.

"See why I like her?" Aggie asked him, returning from the kitchen with a large, steaming bowl of spaghetti sauce. She placed it on the table. Warm garlic bread followed. She gestured them to sit. "Nothing fancy," Aggie pronounced with gusto. "Just something to fill you up and stick to your ribs for a while."

MacKenzie looked at the offering, her mind hungry, her stomach starting to rise in rebellion.

Aggie indicated a small crystal bowl beside MacKenzie's place setting. "I think you might like to put that on your spaghetti before you add the sauce," she told her.

It was ginger, she could tell by the scent. The woman had thought of everything. Mentally, MacKenzie blessed her.

She raised her eyes to Quade, but he was busy cutting the loaf of bread in thirds. She quickly sprinkled the golden spice over her small serving of spaghetti.

Aggie eyed the small portion, her generous mouth frowning in vague disapproval. She picked up a serving fork and added a third more spaghetti to MacKenzie's plate, then covered it in more sauce. "Don't worry about eating me out of house and home. There's plenty more of that on the stove."

Gamely, MacKenzie took her first mouthful. The moment she began to chew, her taste buds were tantalized. A sound of pleasure escaped. She looked at Aggie with awe. "This tastes wonderful."

Aggie looked beyond pleased as she beamed. "Thank you."

MacKenzie knew that a lot of people just paid lip service, thinking they were obligated to because of the host's hospitality. "No, really, I mean it. I know Italian food," she professed. "My father runs Al Dente, an Italian restaurant in Boston. I worked there a couple of summers and—" She stopped abruptly, seeing the expression on Quade's face. "What?"

He shook his head. Talk about coincidence. "I used to eat there sometimes."

MacKenzie looked at him in surprise. "You're from Boston?" There was no telltale accent, but then she had gotten rid of her own years ago. It just took a bit of effort.

"I'm from a lot of places," he corrected, then added, "but Boston's one of them."

She couldn't help wondering if he was just making this up. "Where did you live?"

He told her. Her mouth dropped open. She was vaguely aware of Aggie looking on in amusement. "That's my old neighborhood."

"Small world, isn't it?" Aggie commented. Her voice said that she had already made up her mind as to the answer to the question.

Chapter Six

MacKenzie was barely aware of eating. Her conscious energy was devoted to searching her memory. She was trying to remember if she'd ever bumped into Quade during that small island of years they had been in Boston together, perhaps even served him a meal since he'd said he'd been to her father's restaurant.

But nothing materialized. Boston was a big city and even people in the same neighborhood didn't always know one another. She had the feeling that at no time had Quade Preston ever fallen under the heading of outgoing and friendly. Even in a commune, the man would have found a way to keep to himself.

Unless Aggie had been his neighbor, she thought with a suppressed smile.

"Traveled around a lot, did you?" Aggie asked Quade.

He noticed the smile that MacKenzie struggled to keep under wraps. Why did the sight of it tease his senses that way, making him anticipate seeing it bloom? It made no difference to him one way or another if she smiled, as long as it wasn't at his expense.

"My father's job took us to several different places," he said to his hostess.

For just a moment, he saw Aggie's expression grow wistful. "Must be nice," the woman commented. "Me, I was born and bred right here."

MacKenzie was quick to defend her adopted home. Personally, there was no place she would have rather lived than here.

"Well, if you had to be in only one place," she told Aggie, "New York City would be it. It's got so much to offer." She slid a sidelong glance toward Quade to see if he agreed with her. His expression, as always, was impassive. The man could have posed for a statue with no effort at all. "Can't beat the theater here, or the restaurants. Or the museums," she added quickly.

Her expression grew distant as her own words triggered a memory of the last time she'd gone to the Museum of Natural History. It had been raining outside and she and Jeff had spent hours wandering around the halls, absorbing the past. Talking about the future. She hadn't had a clue that this would be the last time they'd be together.

As if sensing her thoughts were taking her mentally away from the table, Aggie cleared her throat, getting MacKenzie's attention.

"Do you go to the theater?" Aggie asked, her question purposely directed toward Quade.

He didn't like being pinned down about anything, even something as innocuous as the theater. "I just moved here."

Like her Jack Russell terrier, who was sitting in a corner, working away at a soup bone larger than he was, Aggie dug in, ready to outwait Quade for an answer to her question.

"But they had to have some kind of theater where you came from." The woman left the end of the question up in the air, coaxing him to jump in with an answer.

"Maybe they did, but I never went." Anticipating her next question, he added, "Never had the time." He hoped that would be the end of it and that the woman's attention would be redirected toward MacKenzie.

It was, but not in the way he would have appreciated. Aggie shook her head. "All work and no play. We're going to have to change that." She looked at MacKenzie for backup—and a plan of action. "Don't you have access to theater tickets where you work? Good seats?" she added.

Again, her question sounded as if she already knew the answer.

MacKenzie smiled. Because Dakota was in television and the star of a highly rated daytime talk show, getting her hands on things like theater tickets was no problem for her boss/best friend. When you're hot and at the top of your game, it was amazing just how friendly people could be, hoping to catch a little "glow-by-association" from the aura that you cast. And such was the case with Dakota. And what Dakota liked doing best was sharing.

"I'm sure we could get them," she told Aggie. "Any particular one?"

Aggie had a pensive look on her face for a moment as she mentally weeded through the available shows currently playing on Broadway. "I'll have to get back to you on that."

Just for a moment, MacKenzie could have sworn that she heard the strains of the "Matchmaker" song from *Fiddler on the Roof* playing in the background. The woman was trying much too hard, especially since neither MacKenzie nor, she assumed, Quade were in the market to be "matched."

It was time to set this train on another track. MacKenzie looked at Quade. "How long have you been in research?"

Quade stopped eating, not pleased by having attention drawn to him again. Even as a child, he'd always been at his best when he was left alone to do his work. He never needed the validation that came from having someone paste a gold star on his paper or praise him in front of others. He knew what he was capable of and that suited him just fine. He was happiest competing not against others, but himself. That was where the true sense of accomplishment came from, besting himself, going a little further than he had before.

He looked back at his plate and addressed his words to a strand of spaghetti. "Since before I graduated from medical school."

A conversation with Quade took work, MacKenzie decided, but it was the kind of challenge she liked to undertake. So over the course of the dinner, the conversation eked along, with either Aggie or MacKenzie pulling teeth and Quade responding in one or two sentences. One or two words if he could get away with it.

MacKenzie could just visualize him on Dakota's show with the audience no doubt thinking that somehow their programming had gone into slow motion. But she was undaunted. Besides, she liked finding things out about this mysterious, brooding stranger who had moved in next door, no matter how slow the process.

"So do you like this new facility you're working in?" she asked.

He shrugged, putting down his fork. Aggie had urged two servings on him and he felt as if he was going to explode if he even looked at a third. Eating for him was something he did these days out of necessity, not out of a need to satisfy a craving. Ever since Ellen had died, he ate to live, nothing more. But he had to admit, this had been a rather pleasant experience. If only it hadn't been accompanied by a myriad of never-ending questions.

"It's all right," he allowed. "Although I'm not sure how much longer I'll be there."

MacKenzie looked at him incredulously. Wow, talk about wanderlust. "This is just your first day. You couldn't be that restless, could you?"

"Being restless doesn't have anything to do with it. The program at Wiley Labs is underfunded. If some money isn't allocated from somewhere, and soon, the laboratories might have to close their doors, or at least cut back drastically."

MacKenzie looked at him knowingly. "And the last hired is the first let go."

"Something like that."

He made it sound as if he didn't care one way or another, but MacKenzie figured he had to. A man didn't just pick up and move because he was indifferent to his job. Why was he so reluctant to express any sort of attachment to anything?

Aggie looked at MacKenzie. "Couldn't your friend do something about that?"

It made her uneasy the way Aggie just seemed to know things about her. Granted, her life wasn't exactly a state secret, but Aggie had a way of looking at her and intuiting things not readily known. She'd told Quade where she worked but she hadn't mentioned anything about the show to Aggie. Just as she hadn't mentioned that she was pregnant to the woman. Aggie just knew.

"You're talking about Dakota?" It was a rhetorical question.

"Yes." The look Aggie gave her spoke volumes. The next moment, she was the cherubic woman who had corralled them for dinner. "By the way, once I get my act polished I was thinking I could impose on you to get me a three-minute slot on your show."

Everybody and his brother wanted to be on Dakota's show. But saying no to Aggie would have been like saying no to a beloved grandmother on Christmas morning.

"I'll talk to Dakota," MacKenzie promised. And then the seed Aggie had planted first took root. It was as if MacKenzie heard an echo of Aggie's voice in her head. She looked at Quade suddenly. "You know, Dakota's marvelous with fund-raisers. Maybe she could help

Wiley Memorial raise the money it needs to keep the program running."

A fund-raiser? Quade blinked, stunned. He felt as if he'd just been run over by a steamroller. How had a piece of cast-off information suddenly turned into a strategic plan in the making?

His first inclination was to talk MacKenzie out of it. "I don't—"

If, perhaps, there might have been a chance to stop MacKenzie, there was apparently no stopping Aggie once she got started. The older woman rattled off Dakota's qualifications to run a fund-raiser as if they were her own. "Her grandfather used to be on television years ago and she has a lot of ties to the industry. I don't think there's anyone Dakota doesn't know."

It was the kind of statement that begged for a rejoinder. He gave it. "She doesn't know me," Quade pointed out.

Amusement danced in Aggie's soft blue eyes as she looked at him. "Yet."

The next half hour was given over to discussing the fund-raiser that still only existed in the minds of the two women at the table. And slowly, it began to take on breadth and form.

At every turn, Quade felt as if he were outflanked and outmaneuvered. In truth, there was really no good reason for him to try to resist what they were proposing in the first place. After all, he believed in his work, in what he was trying to do, even if it was hideously ironic. He was searching for a cure for leukemia, the way he'd been all along.

On the exact same disease that had taken Ellen away from him. If that wasn't irony, then he hadn't a clue what the word meant.

"I'll talk to Dakota tomorrow," MacKenzie promised, her voice growing in enthusiasm rather than diminishing. "See what she thinks and if she's amenable—and I've never known her not to be to a worthy cause—then she'll get in touch with the laboratories' directors. She'll give you full credit, of course and then—"

His voice was sharp as he cut into her words. "I don't want it."

MacKenzie stopped abruptly, exchanging looks with the older woman at the table. She didn't understand. "You don't want the fund-raiser?"

"No," he said, finishing his wine. Was it his imagination or did it have an unusually powerful kick for something that was supposed to be only marginally proof? "I don't want the credit."

That still left MacKenzie bewildered and curious. "Why not?"

What he liked even less than sharing his thoughts— outside of work—was explaining himself. "Because it's not necessary."

MacKenzie cocked her head and looked at him. Everyone she knew wanted credit. Sometimes for things they hadn't even done but most definitely for what they had, as long as the credit was good.

And this was good, very good.

"Are you part Navajo?" she asked him abruptly. Now that she thought of it, he had the coloring for it and his cheekbones were gaunt and chiseled.

The question, coming out of nowhere, caught him completely unprepared. A little like the woman who asked it. She seemed to make a habit out of making off-the-wall assumptions. "What?"

"Navajo," she repeated. There was no recognition in his eyes. It was as if she were speaking in a foreign tongue. "Navajo Indians, among others, don't believe that it's polite to compete, to steal the thunder for themselves."

He could identify with that, and even if there was a touch of Native American in him, he wouldn't have known. He was down-to-earth, honest-to-gosh American mutt with so many nationalities mixed up within him he could have been his own one-man UN.

But to say something along those lines would have opened up another two hours' worth of conversation, so he found it safest just to shake his head.

"No, I'm not. I just don't see the point in being singled out."

He noted, with a smattering of what he realized was satisfaction, that he had left MacKenzie speechless.

For at least a couple of seconds.

That helped balance out the feeling that he had somehow fallen down the rabbit hole and hadn't a clue as to how to get back out again. The way he saw it, the older woman seemed to arrange things and then the younger one went to town with it until he felt completely snowed in with rhetoric.

Mentally pausing a moment, Quade couldn't remember ever being in the company of anyone who talked as much, or radiated as much enthusiasm, as this woman he was sitting beside.

He needed to retreat as soon as it was politely feasible. But Quade still didn't get his opportunity until almost an hour later. The three of them had cleared the table. He'd helped out over Aggie's protests because he felt it was the right thing to do and because, with his helping, it got the job done faster and him closer to escaping.

But Aggie had had other plans. Dessert had to be served first. It turned out to be some kind of pie-and-ice-cream concoction that flirted with his taste buds, reminding them that they were alive. Reminding him that once he used to go to restaurants just to eat and just to talk. Back in the days when he'd been with Ellen and in love.

A great deal of time had gone by since then.

Still, he had to admit that whatever Aggie had done with the seemingly simple dessert, it was definitely worth sacrificing another fifteen minutes of his solitude.

Finished, MacKenzie smiled as she pushed away her empty dessert plate. She was tempted to have more, but something told her that if she did, she was in danger of exploding. She hadn't eaten so much since she couldn't remember when. If she kept it up, she'd be double her size in no time. Heaven only knew she was going to be larger soon enough.

"I don't know when I've had a better meal," she told Aggie. The latter beamed as she collected the three plates and utensils. MacKenzie glanced toward Quade, waiting to be seconded.

After a beat, Quade read the look in her eyes correctly and added his voice to the praise. "Me, neither."

Considering his sparse verbiage, his words were practically a testimonial.

Aggie deposited the dishes in the sink and returned looking extremely pleased. "Glad to have the opportunity to fill your bellies with a home-cooked hot meal for a change. Feel free to knock on my door anytime. There's always bound to be something in the refrigerator worth heating up."

He had no idea why, when Aggie uttered the last phrase, his attention was drawn to the petite woman sitting on his left.

The thought that MacKenzie might be worth heating up came out of nowhere, as if it had been spawned in some alien mind because it wasn't the kind of thing he thought of, even on an irregular basis.

As a rule, his mind was focused on research, not reproductive glands. And yet, for some reason, as the evening had worn on, he found himself being drawn toward MacKenzie with small, precise waves of anticipation rolling over him, as if deep down he were waiting for something to happen between them.

He was just tired, he told himself, nothing more. Maybe Aggie had used some kind of ingredient he was allergic to and this was just an odd reaction he was experiencing.

Quade had to leave before Aggie found yet another excuse to keep them here. He rose to his feet. "It's late. I'd better get going," he murmured.

MacKenzie glanced at her watch. It was past ten and she had to be in early tomorrow. Where had the time gone?

"Oh God, me, too." Gaining her feet, she kissed

Aggie's cheek and gave the woman a hug that came from the heart. "I had a wonderful time and thank you for everything."

Pleasure danced in the woman's bright blue eyes as she released MacKenzie. "Don't mention it." And then she turned toward Quade, beckoned him toward her. "C'mon, I promise I won't bite. Remember, a hug is a good thing." And then, as she embraced him, Aggie whispered in his ear, "You really do need to loosen up, dear. You'll feel better for it."

Quade stepped back, looking at her uncertainly. Aggie only smiled and winked.

Definitely a very odd woman, he decided, presiding over what had been a very odd evening for him. He'd spent more time in the woman's house and company than he had in anyone's for a very long time, his family included.

He wondered if Aggie was going to make a habit of waylaying him when he came home, the way she'd done this evening. Initially he'd tried to demur, but the woman had sweetly, albeit stubbornly, refused to take no for an answer.

Ultimately, he'd agreed to the woman's invitation because, oddly enough, he was hungry, not to mention tired, and the thought of making the effort to call a take-out place had not appealed to him. To his way of thinking, Aggie had won by default.

But, pleasant though the woman might be, he was not about to let this happen again. He wanted nothing more than just to keep to himself.

Aggie escorted them to the door. Her kindly eyes

washed over both. MacKenzie couldn't shake the impression that the woman saw something that MacKenzie couldn't.

But she was tired and her mind was wandering, she decided.

"Good night. See you two later," Aggie said just before she closed the door.

You two. As if they were a set. MacKenzie shook her head. What was she doing, letting her mind drift like that? She was already part of a set. A mother-and-baby set. She had no intention of being part of anything else for a very long time. There was already too much on her plate.

The night air was damp as it wrapped itself around her. Or was it just that she was suddenly feeling alone? MacKenzie wasn't sure and pushed the thought away as best she could.

She stifled a shiver.

"Cold?" he asked.

"I should have brought a shawl," she admitted. "At least we don't have a long walk home." To her surprise, he took off his jacket and draped it around her shoulders. "Is that the doctor in you coming out?"

"Seemed like the thing to do."

The words were barely audible. And somehow sexy because of the low tone.

She shook herself free, wondering just what had come over her. Maybe it was knowing about the baby, about what lay ahead of her that made her feel vulnerable and open to impossible thoughts that hadn't a chance in hell of ever happening.

Trying to rouse herself, she looked at Quade. "I meant what I said about talking to Dakota. I can almost guarantee that she'd been willing to help you get a fundraiser together."

"That would be good," he commented, not knowing what else to say. He was acutely aware that, beyond the strains of the city that echoed all around them, he could hear MacKenzie breathing. It had a very odd effect on him.

Odd. That was the word for tonight, he thought again. Odd for a variety of reasons, not the least of which was that for the first time since he'd found himself alone, he had become aware of another human being's gender.

He quickened his pace, wanting to get home and shut the door on whatever it was that he was experiencing.

The last time MacKenzie walked across it, the pavement between his apartment and hers had been completely looking-glass smooth. How a crack came to be there she had no idea.

She had even less of an idea how the narrow, three-inch heel of her left shoe got caught in the small space.

What MacKenzie was very aware of was that one moment she was walking—the next she was pitching forward and about to fall.

Chapter Seven

Quade's reflexes had always been razor sharp.

When he had been very young and given to optimism, he had wanted to become a professional ballplayer. At first he'd quietly join in any ongoing neighborhood game. His phenomenal hand-eye coordination, not to mention his batting prowess, was well known in the area and he became much sought after. His playing ability flourished and with it his daydreams.

Until an extremelys mature sense of reality struck, also at an early age, and he realized that the odds of reaching the majors were incredibly small. He put away his bat and glove and turned his attention toward more attainable goals. But his years of playing off and on served to keep his reflexes in top form.

His instincts were keen. Automatic.

When he heard the sharp intake of breath beside him, Quade reacted. Twisting, he caught MacKenzie before he even realized she was falling.

She felt like an idiot, a clumsy idiot.

But more than that, she felt something warm move through her, like a hot desert wind sweeping along the sand on a sultry day. Except that it wasn't quite summer yet and New York City weather was obstinately clinging to memories of a clammy spring.

The lights in the courtyard were spaced so that an occasional shadow could creep in. MacKenzie found herself half in shadow, half in light and completely in the dark as to what was going on inside of her. Or why she felt like melting into the strong arms that had closed around her. He was her knight in slightly tarnished armor, saving her if not from a fate worse than death, then at least from a terribly embarrassing one.

For a second, it seemed as if time had stood still, even though her heart made up for it by hammering twice as hard as it was accustomed to.

Something was happening to her. And then she realized that her feet were off the ground. He'd caught her so fast, so hard, he'd lifted her into his arms.

Her face was inches from his.

His lips were inches from hers.

And something within her leaped out of nowhere, wanting to close the gap.

Begging to close it.

Their eyes met and held as if some force were compelling them to look at one another, unable to look away, unable to look anywhere else.

She wanted him to kiss her.

He was no one to her and she no one to him, but she wanted him to kiss her so badly. Right now, more than anything in the world, she wanted to feel desirable. Wanted to feel something for someone, even lust if that was all that was available.

She didn't even try to explore why.

It didn't make any sense to Quade. He'd all but become a monastic friar ever since he'd buried his wife and his heart in that churchyard over eighteen months ago. At first, to get himself from one end of the day to the other, he'd spent the day in search of his sanity. Most of the time, he couldn't find it.

Then gradually, as he reclaimed his life, he began to look for a purpose, a reason to continue breathing in a world without Ellen. He'd found his purpose, his excuse for living, in his work.

It was enough.

Never in any of that time had he looked for a woman, for companionship, for that rare, head-spinning sense of belonging that he'd so fleetingly found in loving Ellen.

He'd come to think of himself as autonomous. Someone who had no need of companionship. So much so that his family had despaired about him, but he'd made his peace with his solitude. He didn't need anyone to make him complete. Being in love had been just a small, wondrous part of his life, but it was over.

So why then did he want to close his arms more tightly around this woman? Why did he want to press his mouth against hers, taste her on his lips? And why, in heaven's name, did he have this sudden urge to feel her softness against him?

All right, physical desires were a natural thing, but as far back as he could remember, he had never been one to be ruled by his hormones, not even during those wildly erratic stages of puberty. So why this sudden flash, this strong sense of attraction? Of *desire,* for lack of a better word?

It was a backlash, he decided, nothing more than a momentary glitch in time where all the things he'd felt during his years with Ellen had swept over him, demanding a resurgence.

There wasn't going to be one.

Very slowly, Quade caught hold of himself and drew his head back. He released her even more slowly, peering at her to make sure she wasn't going to sink to the ground or something equally unexpected.

"You okay?" he wanted to know. His voice was deep, low, like the distant rumble of thunder. The lightning had already struck.

"I'm fine," MacKenzie lied, feeling like the survivor of some kind of emotional earthquake.

Struggling not to appear as shaken as she felt, MacKenzie looked down at her shoe. The heel hadn't broken off. It appeared to be still intact. Which was more than she could say about herself, she thought ruefully. Again, she could feel the flush of embarrassment sweeping over her.

"Where did that crack come from?" she muttered, seeing it for the first time.

He shrugged dismissively as he made a calculated guess.

"Ground's probably shifting. The subway's not too far away from here." He'd seen an entrance just on the next block. "The constant rattle of passing trains..." Quade's voice drifted away.

"That must be it," MacKenzie agreed quickly, wanting only to escape into her apartment and somehow put a lid on what was going on inside of her until she had it under control again. Hopefully soon. She took a deep breath, attempting to clear her head. "Thanks."

He began to take a step back toward his own apartment. "For what?"

A tiny cloud of calm descended over her and she flashed a smile at him. "For having great reflexes."

"Oh, that."

He'd thought that maybe she was thanking him for not kissing her. Because unless the woman was utterly blind and clueless, she had to have seen that kissing her was exactly what was foremost on his mind.

What was still foremost on his mind, he admitted silently.

"Glad to have been there," Quade heard himself responding.

Talk about a lame comeback, he thought, annoyed at his lack of wit and clarity. But then, language had never been a real tool for him. What he lacked in articulate skills, he more than made up for with his mental acumen. He was a thinker, not a talker.

MacKenzie stood before the door she'd unlocked but hadn't opened yet, reluctant to go inside. Confusion ran riot within her. She was relieved that Quade hadn't kissed her just then and yet, at the same time, she felt somehow bereft.

Cheated.

And then, while her heart still throbbed, impulse kicked in. Impulse that was responsible for so much that had happened in her life. Impulse had had her going to a college other than the one everyone else had expected her to go to. It had been at this other college that she'd met and hooked up with the woman who was to become her best friend in the world, not to mention the source of all her future job opportunities.

MacKenzie had always been a great believer in impulse.

So when it swept over her, reinforcing the feelings that were still vibrating inside of her, MacKenzie moved away from her doorway. She took the few steps to his, reached up and took Quade's face in her hands and then kissed him.

Hard and quickly.

Leaving herself feeling like someone who had just been sucked into a vortex.

He was looking at her, a stunned expression on his face.

Was he dazed, as well? she wondered. Because God knew that was what she was feeling right now.

"That's for saving me from scraped knees, injured pride and worse," she told him, shoving his jacket into his hands.

With that, MacKenzie made her escape, quickly seeking safety behind her door.

Before she was tempted to kiss him again.

Because his lips had been firm, but yielding, and

that one taste had definitely unraveled her, making her want to go back for more. Her pulse still hummed as she wove her way through the dark into the rear of the apartment and her bedroom.

She doubted she was going to get much sleep tonight, no matter what kind of a bill of goods she tried to sell herself about the origin of her impulse.

Quade stood stone still halfway between her door and his. Lost between stunned and something else, what he wasn't quite sure of. All he knew was that after MacKenzie had surprised him with that kiss, he wanted to sweep her back into his arms and kiss her himself.

Really kiss her.

Transference, he told himself. That was all that it was. Transference.

That was what he was doing now, he told himself. Transferring all those residual feelings he was still experiencing, the ones with Ellen's name on them that were still wandering around aimlessly inside of him. Without Ellen around, they had nowhere to go.

By now, he would have thought that they would have faded out of existence instead of haunting him like this. Or worse, suddenly aiming themselves toward someone else.

He didn't want someone else.

He wanted to be left alone.

Loving someone was not worth the risk, the pain that was attached to it, its advent as inevitable as the sunset each evening.

Swallowing an oath, Quade let himself into his apartment and shut the door firmly behind him.

* * *

The following day, one thought gnawing away at her, MacKenzie tried to choose her time well and waited until Dakota was alone in her dressing room. Knocking softly, she paused before opening the door and peering inside.

"You busy?"

Dakota was sitting curled up on the small, dark brown love seat, a legal-size white lined pad on her lap. Glancing up, she flashed MacKenzie a smile before looking back to the pad.

"No more than usual. What's up?"

MacKenzie shut the door behind herself. "Remember when you said the other day that if I needed something, I could come to you?"

In the middle of going over her notes for a rather tough interview she was facing on today's show, Dakota abruptly stopped and looked up. There was an uncertain note in MacKenzie's voice that she wasn't used to hearing. MacKenzie usually barreled right through life.

"Anything," Dakota reiterated, not knowing what to anticipate, except that whatever MacKenzie asked her for, she was going to say yes. She set the pad aside and patted the seat next to her. "What do you need?"

Sitting down like someone who expected to spring to her feet at any moment, MacKenzie began to feel Dakota out. "How busy are you?"

It struck Dakota as an odd question, given that MacKenzie was part of this process. Of late, life seemed to have thrown itself into the fast-forward mode. And it was only getting worse.

"Relative to what? Santa Claus fifteen minutes be-fore he has to take off on Christmas Eve? I guess I'm a little less busy than that." Dakota sighed, thinking of the schedule that she'd jotted down for herself that morn-ing, the way she did every morning. Scheduling every-thing was the only way she'd found that allowed her successfully to juggle her flourishing career and her very new, very fulfilling home life. "I've got fifteen, maybe twenty minutes to spare between now and Easter," she judged. "Why?"

"Then you probably wouldn't have any time for a fund-raiser, would you?"

Dakota stared at her. Her eyes narrowed as her interest piqued. "This conversation is not going where I thought it was going. I thought you were going to ask me to be your birthing coach, or fund a college education for little who's-its, or—a fund-raiser?" she echoed, the full import of MacKenzie's request sinking in. "A fund-raiser for who?"

MacKenzie began to backtrack. Every time she was excited, she tended to trip over her own tongue, which could never keep up with her racing mind. "Ever hear of Wiley Memorial Research Laboratories?"

There were a great many charities associated with the people who traveled in Dakota's circle. "Yes, I've heard of them. What about the institute?"

Normally, MacKenzie had no trouble talking to Dakota about anything. They'd been friends for over ten years, since the first day they had each set foot in the UCI dorm room and instantly clicked. But she knew that there would be questions once she framed this re-quest and she just didn't feel like fielding them. She blamed her fluctuating hormones that were bobbing up and down like corks in a riptide. The same hormones that had all but cheered when she'd kissed Quade last night.

She felt as if she owed this to him.

"Well," she began slowly, picking her words as if she were trying to select the best specimens from a freshly harvested crop of strawberries, "it seems that they're in financial difficulties and they might have to close down some really important research programs—"

Dakota was having trouble following this. "And they came to you?" Ordinarily, tickets to fund-raisers came to her directly, not through MacKenzie.

MacKenzie ran her tongue along her lower lip. "Not exactly. The guy who moved in next door—"

Dakota sat up, her body instantly at attention. "A guy moved in next door?"

MacKenzie stopped and gave Dakota an exasperated look. That a male was occupying the apartment next door was beside the point. Kind of.

"Dakota, keep up," she instructed.

Things were getting clearer. Dakota grinned, getting comfortable. She tucked one leg beneath her. "For that, I need to be filled in."

"There's nothing to fill in," she said dismissively. But because Dakota was apparently waiting for more, she reluctantly added, "The apartment next door to mine has a new tenant. He works for Wiley Labs."

The interviewer in her kicked in and Dakota threw out questions, wanting more details. "Works for Wiley Labs how? As a maintenance man? A guard? A—"

"He's a research physician."

Dakota's face lit up with approval. "Oh, he's a doctor."

It took everything MacKenzie had not to throw up her hands. "My God, Dakota, stop sounding like some kind of caricature of an overprotective mother trying to marry off her spinster daughter."

Dakota pretended to be contrite. "Sorry." And then her face lit up again as she continued her quest for more information. "So how did you find out that Wiley Labs is running low on funding?"

"He mentioned it."

Dakota frowned slightly. She wasn't accustomed to having to resort to pulling teeth in order to get information out of MacKenzie. Ordinarily, MacKenzie talked nonstop with no encouragement. She couldn't help wondering if this new side to MacKenzie was somehow the result of her pregnancy.

"Just like that? He knocks on your door, says 'Hey, I'd like to borrow a cup of sugar, unless you've got some extra funding in your pantry, and then I'd like that, instead.'"

MacKenzie blew out a breath, feeling irritated and feeling guilty to boot that she was. "No, he said it over dinner—"

Dakota jumped on the word just as MacKenzie knew she would. "Dinner? You went out to dinner with him?"

"Just over to Aggie's place."

"Aggie." Another new name. Dakota knew it might seem a tad unreasonable, but she wasn't accustomed to being a stranger in her best friend's life. "MacKenzie, have you been leading a secret life since I got married? You used to tell me when you lost a button on your blouse, now I had to ask all sorts of questions to find out that you're pregnant."

MacKenzie hadn't meant to distance herself from Dakota. She truly loved her like the sister she'd always prayed for when she was younger. It was just that, with this new direction her life had suddenly taken, everything was on its ear. The sight of sunrise even irritated her.

She knew she was being unreasonable. Dakota was just trying to help. MacKenzie knew she could count on her. That was why she'd approached the woman with this to begin with.

MacKenzie offered her best friend an apologetic smile.

"Okay, I'll start printing a daily news bulletin about my life, but could we get back to the question, please?"

"Sure." Dakota leaned forward, all ears and interest. "So, what's he like, this new neighbor with the needy laboratories?"

"My question, not yours," MacKenzie emphasized. Then, to make amends, she tossed Dakota a bone. "He's cute in a dark, brooding sort of way."

"Oh, an antihero."

It was as good a description as any, MacKenzie thought. She talked quickly before Dakota could get another question in.

"I told him that you were a wizard when it came to putting together a fund-raiser and that maybe you could help. Otherwise, the program he's working on might wind up being cut."

"Can't have that." Dakota saw the exasperated look making a reappearance on MacKenzie's face. "I'm serious." Off the top of her head, she knew there were no islands of time readily available to her, but she could always make one. That was one of the things she was good at, one of the things her mother had taught her how to do. "Okay, give me the particulars—who, what, when," she clarified. "I'll see what I can do."

MacKenzie realized that she'd put the cart before the horse. These were all things she should have found out before coming to Dakota. But, she had a feeling that Quade might not have gone to his employer to get the information until he had a firm commitment from Dakota that she was onboard.

"I don't have them yet," MacKenzie admitted.

Dakota took the information in stride. "Then go back and get them." She picked up the pad again, placing it on her lap. "It'll give you an excuse to knock on his door."

Thank God she hadn't said anything about last night's kiss, MacKenzie thought. Dakota was going to town on next to nothing. If MacKenzie had said something about kissing him, Dakota would be out there picking out party favors for the wedding reception. "I don't need an excuse."

Amusement rose in Dakota's eyes. "Oh, it's that kind of relationship."

MacKenzie sighed deeply, feeling as if she'd run this track before. "It isn't any kind of relationship."

Tossing the pad aside a second time, Dakota rose to her feet and took hold of her friend's shoulders, looking her squarely in the eye.

"Zee, if it wasn't any kind of relationship, you wouldn't be sporting that very interesting pink color on your cheeks."

MacKenzie shrugged off her hold. "That's just because it's hot in here."

"It's the same temperature it's always been." And then Dakota suddenly looked at the cameo around MacKenzie's neck. And smiled. "When did he move in?"

"Tuesday," MacKenzie told her. Dakota was grinning broadly, as if she'd just landed the guest of the year on her show. "What?"

Dakota ran her fingertip along the outline of the cameo. "Tuesday," she echoed. "That was the day after I gave you the necklace."

That didn't mean anything, MacKenzie thought, refusing to believe that the legend was remotely true. "I also met Aggie that day."

Dakota cocked her head, curious. "And just what is an Aggie?"

MacKenzie remembered Aggie's comment about wanting five minutes on Dakota's show. She might as well lay the groundwork for that, too, MacKenzie thought. "Aggie is a seventy-two year old woman who has decided to change careers and become a stand-up comedian."

The very idea fired Dakota's imagination. She loved stories like this. "Now her I'd like to meet–" she looked at MacKenzie pointedly "—too."

MacKenzie deliberately ignored the *too*. "That can be arranged."

"Great. Now, get me the name of the head of Wiley

Labs and I'll see what we can do to keep your guy working."

MacKenzie tried again, although she knew it was close to hopeless. Once Dakota had made up her mind, dynamite couldn't dislodge it. "He's not my guy, Dakota."

"Whatever you say." Dakota sat down again, picking up the pad for the third time. "Now if I don't finish going over these notes I made for myself, we're not going to have a show today."

Giving MacKenzie another wide grin, coupled with a high sign, Dakota went back to studying her notes.

MacKenzie withdrew from the dressing room, an entire houseboat of mixed feelings bobbing and weaving through the choppy waters of her soul.

Chapter Eight

For perhaps the first time in a long time, MacKenzie became aware of how fast-paced her life was. Maybe it was because right now, because of the baby, she felt as if she were moving in slow motion and had gotten sucked in by the whirling hurricane that was her career.

Since things had stepped up, she didn't get a chance to reconnect with Quade until Saturday morning. In a way, that was all to the good because she needed a little time to realign her thinking and her emotions. She wanted no repeat performances, spontaneous or not, of what had happened between their two doors the other night.

With an eye out to May sweeps, she'd had to put in extra hours trying to line up special guests for Dakota. This while attending the endless staff meetings that populated each day. Staff meetings where a great deal of talking occurred, but very little progress and next to no resolution.

As far as MacKenzie was concerned, she was in the greatest business in the world, but there were times when being part of that world really wore her out. Especially when she faced the beginning of each day feeling as if she had all the untapped energy of an overcooked strand of spaghetti.

Still, she did manage to get over to Quade's door a total of two times in the latter half of the week. Both times she'd rang the bell, there'd been no answer. A belated glance toward his parking space showed her that his car was missing, as well. Quade was either putting in even worse killer hours than she was, or he was out there, familiarizing himself with the city's nightlife.

Given what she'd seen of his personality, MacKenzie figured it was more likely the former than the latter.

And then on Saturday, after Dakota had called her on the phone to ask yet again if she'd gotten a chance to speak to "the hunk next door" about the particulars behind the needed fund-raiser, MacKenzie ventured out of her apartment to try again.

As she did so, it occurred to her that she hadn't seen Aggie around lately, either. She wondered what the woman was up to and decided that if she had the energy, maybe she'd drop in on her later.

She glanced to see if Quade's car was in the carport. The vintage automobile sat quietly in the spot beside her cherry-red Mustang.

Okay, so unless he'd taken the subway somewhere,

he should be home. Marching up to his door, she rang the bell.

There was no answer.

MacKenzie looked at her watch. It was well past nine o'clock. Most people, other than graveyard security guards, didn't sleep in past that time on a Saturday. For working people, Saturday represented the one day that they could try to cram all the errands and responsibilities that piled up during the other five. Sundays were pretty much for recuperating.

MacKenzie tried again, leaning a little on the bell this time. There was still no answer.

The third time, she resorted to knocking. Hard. Though he didn't seem the type, she thought that maybe he *was* still in bed and needed to be summarily roused. Knocking got her nowhere. Short of pounding a doubled-up fist on the surface, she'd made as much noise as she was capable of making.

She wondered if anything was wrong and decided that perhaps her "delicate" condition had made her a little paranoid. He was probably just a sound sleeper. A very sound sleeper.

Giving up, she turned away. About to return to her own apartment, MacKenzie heard the door opening behind her. When she looked over her shoulder, she saw Quade standing in the doorway. He wore a paint-splattered work shirt, equally christened jeans and held a roller in the hand that wasn't on the doorknob.

There was something very rugged and earthy-looking about him.

She squelched the thought, telling herself she was reacting like a dieter to a hot fudge sundae. She refused to entertain any other explanation for the sudden, light-headed feeling that was undulating through her.

Her brows drew together as she looked at the roller again. "You're painting."

He found the bemused, slightly confused expression on her face oddly appealing. "What was your first clue?"

She ignored the sarcastic tone in his voice. She hadn't come here to wrestle verbally with him.

Wrestling might be fun, a small voice in the recesses of her mind whispered.

She wondered if hallucinations were part of first-time pregnancies.

MacKenzie nodded at the roller he was holding. "Isn't management supposed to do that for you when you first move in?"

"The old tenant moved out Saturday. I needed a place in a hurry because I was starting my job and had to have somewhere to stay. Management offered to paint the apartment after I moved in, but I didn't want to come home to find strangers crawling around my place."

No, she thought, he wouldn't have. "Privacy issues, huh?"

"No 'issues.'" He thoroughly disliked that word. Something was a problem or it wasn't. *Issues* was a word to describe magazines, like the latest issue of *People* or *Time*. But mentioning that would probably embroil him in some kind of long, convoluted debate he had no intention of getting into. So he merely said, "I'm just not keen on strangers."

Was it her imagination, or was he looking at her pointedly for some reason? Paranoia again, she decided.

Moving past Quade, she peered into the living room. It was half yellow, half soft blue, the same color on his paint roller.

MacKenzie nodded her approval. "Nice choice," she told him.

Still standing by the door, he shifted from one foot to the other, impatient to get back to what he was doing. Impatient to have her gone. Any way he looked at it, she was a distraction.

"Thanks. Look," he said, opening the door farther, a silent invitation, "I'm kind of busy right now—"

This man was not in the running for host of the year, she thought, amused as she turned back to face him. "I came to tell you that Dakota needs to know the particulars."

"Particulars?" He had no idea what she was talking about, or who for that matter. Was this some vague reference to some kind of news story she'd heard about one of the Dakota states? He hadn't a clue and, frankly, he was in no mood to play games. He had only the space of today to finish painting his apartment. Tomorrow was reserved for the lab. Until the money ran out, people in his department were pulling double shifts.

Looking at him, MacKenzie realized that he was drawing a complete blank. The man had too much on his mind, she decided.

"Regarding the fund-raiser. We talked about it," she reminded him, enunciating the words slowly so that they could register. But there was no light of recognition coming into his eyes. She gave him another hint. "At Aggie's table when she had us there for dinner the other night." His expression didn't change. She blew out a breath. The paint fumes had obviously gotten to his brain, blotting out the part that was reserved for short-term memory. "You said that Wiley Labs was under-funded and—"

Now he remembered who Dakota was. It wasn't a place, it was a person. The woman MacKenzie had said she worked for. And then he looked at her in surprise. "You actually asked her?"

"I said I would." And then her smile faded a little. Had she misread signals? "Why—didn't you want me to?"

He hadn't had any thoughts about it one way or an-other. He's just assumed that it was one of those throw-away lines, like "We'll talk," and "Let's do lunch." He hadn't actually expected her to follow through.

The idea of a fund-raiser definitely had its merits. It might actually buy Wiley Labs some time, provided that it was successful. "No, I'm just surprised that she'd actually be willing to help."

He sounded so distant, so disengaged from the world that existed around her. She suddenly felt sorry for him. "Why? Don't people help each other in the world you live in?"

Because he felt like an idiot walking around with a roller in his hand, Quade walked inside his apartment and retired it to the tray he'd been using. It still held a generous amount of light blue paint in it.

"Yes, but usually for a reason." In his experience,

most people didn't do anything unless there was something in it for them.

MacKenzie came to Dakota's defense. "Well, Dakota
has a reason. She likes to help. Dakota has always been
easily the most generous soul I've ever known. She
grew up in show business, where people were always
running off to do something for charity when they
weren't collecting together talent to fly overseas and entertain the troops stationed in various foreign countries.
It's what she does," she explained.

MacKenzie looked around. He hadn't gotten around
to opening any more boxes than the one she'd seen him
tackling at the beginning of the week. The remaining
boxes were clustered around the existing furniture.
Everything was pulled together into the center of the
room like members of a wagon train circling in anticipation of a hostile attack. From the looks of it, he had
a great deal of work ahead of him. Paint-wise, only the
kitchen was done.

"Got an extra roller or brush?" she asked suddenly.

He'd bought two. He liked being prepared just in
case something went wrong with one. "Yes," he admitted slowly, eyeing her. "Why?"

"I'm with the local hardware store and I'm taking in-
ventory for them," she quipped. "Why do you think? To
help you paint."

He frowned. "I don't remember asking."

"Good, because if you did, you'd be hallucinating."
Rather than wait for him to produce it, MacKenzie
looked around and spotted the extra roller, still wrapped
in plastic, lying on the kitchen table. Pleased with her-

self, she took off her jacket and placed it on the back of a chair. She rolled up her sleeves before going over to the roller and ripping off the plastic.

He felt as if he'd just been invaded. "There's no need for you to do that," Quade told her as he followed her into the kitchen.

"Trust me, there is. After doing nothing but thinking all week, I really need to do something physical to help me balance it all out. You'd be doing me a favor."

He couldn't figure out if she was being serious or not. All he knew was that she was wearing a sweater that nearly matched the walls he was painting. The garment caressed her curves and drew his eye to the low neckline. He would really be better off if she weren't here, distracting him.

"I sincerely doubt that," he told her, placing his hand on the roller and ready to take it out of her hand.

Except that she was holding on.

He saw amusement enter her eyes. "Why do you make it so hard for people to be nice to you?"

"Maybe it's because I don't want to owe anyone."

Or form bonds, because bonds broke. And when they did, it hurt too much. It was better his way. If you moved through life in a solitary fashion, you didn't expect anything. No expectations, no disappointments. It was as simple as that.

Or so he thought.

But apparently she had other thoughts on the matter. With a snap of her wrist, she pulled the roller out of his hand.

"There's no charge, no tab. I'll owe you, okay?"

His eyes swept over her. "You'll get paint on your clothes."

MacKenzie looked down for his benefit. "These were going into the rag bin soon anyway. They might as well accomplish something useful before they go."

He blew out a breath. "Have an answer for everything, don't you?"

"In my line of work, it helps to be able to cover your back at all times."

Resigned to having her help him, at least for a little while, Quade popped the lid off the can of paint he'd been using and poured a little more into the tray. He took her words at face value. "This Dakota, she a hard taskmaster?"

"Dakota?" she echoed incredulously. Nothing could have been further from the truth. "Dakota Delaney is the sweetest, most generous person in the whole world. I was talking about management."

She waited for him to set the paint container aside. The second he was finished pouring paint into the tray, she immersed her roller, moving it around until the last shred of pink disappeared beneath an ocean of light blue.

MacKenzie carefully removed the excess before applying the roller to the wall. "Since I'm shorter than you, I'll take the bottom of the walls. You take the top."

The division of labor sat well with him. There was no way he would have allowed her to climb up on the ladder he'd borrowed from the super. "You give orders like a general."

MacKenzie laughed as she selected a section of wall and got started. "Hey, Napoleon was approximately my height."

She was right, she thought as she spread with growing gusto the color along the wall. It *did* feel good to do something with her hands, to let her mind drift, emptied of strategy meetings and schedules.

Needing more paint, she crossed back to the tray and dipped her roller in. She glanced toward him. Quade was using a pole extension, his strokes reaching all the way up almost to the ceiling. For a second, she watched him move. He was graceful, she thought and wondered if he knew that. Probably not. He didn't strike her as someone who paid much attention to himself, only to the details of whatever he was doing.

She thought of what he'd just said. "Was that your polite way of saying I'm bossy?"

"Just an observation." Looking in her direction, he saw that MacKenzie had stopped painting and was looking at him. Now what? He raised his brow in a silent query directed at her. Missing the peace and quiet that had been here only minutes ago.

"You can smile," she said.

"What?"

"Just now, when I asked you if you were saying that I was bossy, I saw a glimmer of a smile on your lips." She grinned, doing something very odd, very unsettling to his stomach. "Nice," she pronounced.

Impatience clawed at him. Trouble was, he wasn't exactly sure just what it was that he was being impatient about. The work was getting done, perhaps even faster than he'd anticipated. And he had nowhere else to be, nothing else to accomplish today. So why did he feel like a man about to miss his train connection, the last one out for that day?

"What are you talking about?" he heard himself all but snapping. Why was she babbling about smiles? If she wanted to help him paint, then she should paint, not talk. Not distract.

She placed her feelings in a full sentence. "You look nice when you smile."

Perversely, he pulled his lips into a frown. "I wasn't aware that I was smiling."

She expected nothing less. It was there and then that she decided she was going to find out his story. Just because he was guarding it so zealously. "You were. And you should do it more often. Doesn't make you look nearly as scary."

About to apply more paint to his roller, he stopped a second and glanced at her. And then moved his roller back and forth in the paint. If he let her, she was going to make him come to a grinding halt.

"You think I look scary?" he asked.

"Definitely." She turned her back to him so that he couldn't see the grin playing on her lips. "I think all the dogs and small children under four feet in the neighborhood have all scattered and run away."

"Doesn't seem to have scared you off."

"I'm not under four feet," she pointed out.

Something else to lament, he thought. Slapping his roller against the wall, Quade attacked it with a vengeance.

* * *

The conversation for the next two hours continued in the same nebulous, scattered way. Quade found himself growing progressively more entertained and amused. The annoyance he'd wrapped around himself as almost a shield was dissipating and fading.

He had no idea what to make of it, only that he felt naked.

At one point, he turned around after receiving no answer to one of his very few questions. MacKenzie had suddenly turned a very translucent shade of white. Rather than set it down somewhere, he dropped his roller to the newspaper-covered floor and hurried over to her.

"What's the matter?"

The room was spinning and she had no idea why. All she knew was that she wasn't going to faint like some stereotypical pregnant woman. That would have been too unreal.

Yet she was having trouble hanging on to her surroundings. An encroaching blackness was threatening to swallow everything up. She was aware of his hands around her, forcing her to the floor.

A wolf in research physician's clothing? Had she made a stupid mistake, trusting him?

She struggled to sit up, feeling weak. It took no effort to keep her down.

"Lie still, damn it."

"You're going to have to improve your foreplay," she said with effort.

"Foreplay?" The situation was worse than he

thought. The woman was delirious. Had the paint fumes gotten to her? But the window was open. It made no sense—and neither did she.

He felt her pulse. It was beating like a percussion soloist. "Do you want to go to the emergency room?"

His words were coming to her from some distance. She struggled to get closer to them and farther from the abyss.

"You're a doctor… Doctor me…."

"Delirious," he pronounced out loud.

"Air," she told him, grasping onto consciousness and holding on for all she was worth. "I just need some air. Paint fumes—"

He'd breathed in the same paint and felt nothing except for a small, vague headache behind his eyes. But then, he knew that people reacted differently to the same stimulus. He did as she asked, crossing to the large bay window that looked out on the courtyard and pushed it all the way open instead of just partially. A cool breeze immediately pushed its way in, its long, thin probing fingers moving everywhere.

She took a deep breath. The darkness around her receded as if it had never existed. She started to sit up, only to find that he was still pushing her back down.

"Quade, I can't just lie here like a strange conversation piece. You're going to have to let me sit up sometime."

He frowned, taking her pulse again. It had settled down considerably. And her color was returning. He sat back on his heels. "What the hell was that all about?"

There was no way she was going to tell him the

truth. Instead, she clung to her story. "I already told you, it had to be the paint fumes."

"C'mon, I'll walk you home," he offered.

"I'm fine now," she insisted. "And there's not that much left to do."

"Good, then I can finish it myself."

"And rob me of the pleasure of looking at a job well done? I don't think so." Using his shoulder for leverage, she pushed herself up to her feet.

"Have you always been this pigheaded?"

"I prefer to think of it as attractively determined."

He gave her a look. "The word is pigheaded." Quade ground the words out.

She shrugged casually. "Your place, your rules."

"Then—"

She knew where it was headed before he said anything. "But I am finishing this up with you. How about we compromise? If I get woozy again, you can give me the bum's rush home." She smiled up at him, fluttering her lashes. "Deal?"

He had no choice but to agree. But he watched her for the remaining half hour like a parent afraid his four-year-old was going to dart across the traffic-laden street. He noted that because of that, she got more done than he did.

"Tired?" he asked her when she finally put down her roller.

She rotated her shoulders. "Yes, but in a good way. Sorry about before. Didn't mean to scare you."

He made no comment on her statement, feeling it was best to leave it alone. To deny that she had momentarily frightened him would have been a lie. She'd gotten so pale, as pale as Ellen had been toward the end. It had brought back too many bad memories for him.

He nodded toward the chair in the middle of the room.

"Why don't you sit down—rest? I can order a pizza." Even as he heard himself make the offer, he was stunned to realize that it was coming from him. She was about to leave and he was actually postponing her exit rather than encouraging it. Maybe the paint fumes had affected him, too.

It was tempting. A very small part of her still felt like collapsing, though she felt a lot stronger. It was all due to the pregnancy, she guessed. Ever since its onset, she was constantly experiencing all these highs and lows. Energy would no sooner spike then vanish, sending her into some pit or another until she pulled herself out again, only to be bowled over by another surge.

She eyed the chair, then shook her head. "No, if I do that, I might not be able to dig myself out again."

She weighed, what, maybe a hundred pounds? Probably not. "I don't think I'd have to rent a crane to help you to your feet."

Not yet, anyway, she thought. But soon enough.

"Thank you for sharing that image. No, I'd better just get going." The thought of a hot bubble bath had popped into her head in the last few minutes and now that was all she wanted.

Belatedly he realized he should be walking her out, even though the entire trip was accomplished in less than one heartbeat.

"Thanks for your help," he said, following her to the door.

"Even though I talked your ear off?"

"They're still on," he assured her.

She turned to face him, pretending to check out his ears just to make sure. "I guess they are at that. Don't forget to talk to your boss about the fund-raiser idea," she reminded him.

He nodded. "Right." But as she turned away again, he noticed something. "Hey, hold it."

She stopped abruptly. "What?"

"You have paint on your face."

Was that all? She laughed. "And probably in my hair and everywhere else." Some of it had probably been sustained when he'd placed her on the floor. "What can I say? I really get into anything I do."

The image that brought to mind was not one that had anything to do with painting. Instead, he could suddenly envision her making love. With utter and complete abandon.

He shut down his thoughts. "No, just on your cheek," he told her. Quade fished out a handkerchief. Taking her chin in his hand, he turned her head so that her cheek faced him and began to wipe it. "Don't worry, the handkerchief's clean."

"I wasn't worried." Her voice was soft, low, as the breath inside her lungs slowed to a crawl.

Suddenly aware of what he was doing, and just how intimate it felt, Quade dropped his hand to his side. "It's gone."

MacKenzie looked at him, wondering if that wild

charge of electricity that had suddenly materialized out of nowhere had manifested itself to him, as well, or if she was the only one standing out in the middle of this thunderstorm.

Chapter Nine

"Thank you."

MacKenzie's own words echoed in her ears as she stood looking up at Quade.

If she didn't leave, she was going to make that same mistake again. The one she'd made the night of Aggie's dinner.

Even now, she could feel everything inside her urging her on. Urging her to kiss him again. He was going to think she was some kind of desperate female, never mind the fact that she was pregnant and had no business kissing a man who was not the father of her baby.

Besides, kissing was how this whole thing had originally started, MacKenzie reminded herself, trying vainly to hold her ground. Kissing led to other things and she was in no position to move on to "other things."

There were a thousand reasons for her just to walk out the door—quickly—but not a single one of them could get her to move her feet. They remained glued to the rug. As glued as her eyes were to his.

A small, ragged breath escaped her lips.

Later, when he could look back at this with some measure of sanity, Quade would realize that he was operating on automatic pilot. He really couldn't be blamed for what happened. Something inside of him had risen up, desperate to recapture that small island of time from his past when he had actually felt happy.

When he had felt whole.

He framed MacKenzie's face in his hands and lowered his mouth to hers, reclaiming that island, if only for just a moment.

The instant his lips met hers, he felt a surge flash through him. In its wake came a validation that this wasn't wrong, that this was right.

Inside of him, strange, wonderful sensations were rallying, linking up with his past and the memory of things the way they used to be when he'd felt hope.

She tasted warm, delicious and tantalizing. He urged himself to deepen the kiss, to ride out the wave and discover just how far it would take him.

He was free-falling and the ground was a thousand miles away.

The rush was incredible.

But then the rush vanished. Guilt and fear found their way into his consciousness, banking down the wondrous sensations and shoving them back into the dark recesses where they had been housed.

He drew his head back and looked at her. There was a bemused smile gracing the blurred outline of MacKenzie's lips.

It took effort to speak without sighing. Her toes still felt curled. In a way, she was surprised that the room was still there and that she was still in it. For a moment there, she'd felt airborne.

"I think you just burnt off all the paint that might have been on my body."

The observation was so strange, he found himself laughing. Though she'd aroused some of the same passions inside of him, she was a world apart from Ellen. Heaven knew she hadn't responded to him the way Ellen would have, with a gentle sigh and a silent invitation in her eyes. Humor had never been part of their relationship. They had had warmth and understanding and love, but not humor. To him, Ellen had always felt like a softer, kinder extension of himself.

As for this woman who had spearheaded her way into his life, well, he didn't know what sort of a label to pin to her. He *was* sure that he had no business kissing her like this no matter what his body was begging him to do.

Feeling strangely shaken, Quade stepped back, putting distance between them. But not between the sensations she had drawn out of him. They hadn't been banked down, not completely. And they were reconnoitering for another attack. One he couldn't afford to let happen.

"I didn't mean…" he began, not quite sure what it was he was going to say, only that he wanted to promise her that this wasn't going to happen again. Promise himself that it wasn't going to happen again.

But he didn't get the opportunity.

MacKenzie laid a finger to his lips, stopping him from saying anything else. "Don't spoil it." It was half an entreaty, half an instruction. "It's okay."

Whether she meant that his kiss was okay or his regret over the same, Quade hadn't a clue. He had the feeling he should just walk away and ignore the whole thing. Ignore the stirrings that he felt because that way, he could avoid certain disaster. He'd loved Ellen and loving her was both the best and the worst thing that had ever happened to him. Best because he'd had a piece of paradise, worst because he now knew the difference and was keenly aware of the loss.

MacKenzie pressed her lips together, trying to withdraw gracefully. "Don't forget to ask your boss about having a fund-raiser."

He stared at her for a second, then realized what she was referring to. Not only had he forgotten about the fund-raiser but he'd very nearly forgotten his name, where he was and how he'd come to be there. For a diminutive woman, she packed one hell of a punch.

"Right," he muttered.

Quade barely remembered shutting the door after she left. He was too busy struggling to shut away the feelings that had tried to break free.

Quade didn't get a chance to talk to his superior at Wiley Memorial on Sunday. After briefly meeting him last Tuesday and formally welcoming him to the institute, Adam Petrocelli had taken off for a business conference. Petrocelli's secretary told Quade that he was expected back in the middle of Monday afternoon, but that his schedule was packed with meetings.

Quade made a mental note to take a late lunch on Monday. Though it was completely out of character for him, Quade made it his business to waylay Petrocelli in his office before the man could be called away to the first of a multitude of meetings.

Taking advantage of the fact that Petrocelli's secretary was away from her desk, Quade hurried past it and into the man's inner office.

Adam Petrocelli, an average-looking man in an above-average suit, looked a little surprised to see Quade enter. "Mr. Petrocelli, I'm Dr. Quade Preston" He tried not to seem as uncomfortable as he felt in this new role. But there was a great deal more at stake here than just his comfort.

Even with the name, it appeared to take Petrocelli a moment to remember who Quade was. When the man finally did, he extended a wide paw, grasping Quade's hand and giving it a hearty shake.

"Oh, right, you're the new research physician who started last Tuesday. We met just before I flew to Dallas. So, how are you finding your way around?"

"Fine." Quade had no affinity for small talk because it got in the way of more important things. The only way he knew how to proceed was straight ahead. "I heard rumors that Wiley Memorial was running low on funding and that certain programs were going to have to be cut or reduced."

"And you're worried about your job," Petrocelli surmised. It was no secret that nine years ago, the man had been brought in by Wiley Labs to shore up their beaches. Petrocelli had an MBA and was very good at what he did, managing finances and finding money. He knew a little about medicine, but a great deal about how to make things work financially.

Quade could tell that the man was debating telling him that the rumors were wrong. Quade saved him the trouble.

"No, that's not why I'm here. Dakota Delaney is interested in hosting a fund-raiser for Wiley Labs and I thought you might want to put someone in touch with her."

Petrocelli stared at Quade for a moment, as if digesting what he'd just been told.

"Dakota Delaney?" he echoed, then blinked. "You know Dakota Delaney?"

Quade hadn't meant to give that impression. He wouldn't have known the woman if he'd tripped over her. "Indirectly."

Confusion registered on Petrocelli's face. "How indirectly?"

Quade hurried to give him the complete picture. "Her assistant producer, MacKenzie Ryan, is my next-door neighbor. Actually, she was the one who suggested that Ms. Delaney would be willing to host a fund-raiser when I told her that I'd heard Wiley might be having some financial difficulties."

Admiration lit up Petrocelli's dark brown eyes. "You really roll up your sleeves when you work for a place, don't you?"

Quade had never been thought of as a joiner before, as someone who was part of a team. It was a novel concept for him and not one that was entirely distasteful, given the present situation. "I don't believe in half measures."

Petrocelli made himself comfortable, treating him, Quade noted, as a confidante. That, too, was a new experience for him.

"Thank God for that. Of course I'd welcome her help." Petrocelli smiled broadly, his eyes all but disappearing into the expression. "And any money that something like that could generate." For just a moment, he looked older than his forty-six years. "I just spent the last four days in Dallas with my hat in my hand, begging the Malfi Foundation for more money." Quade knew that the eighty-year-old organization underwrote the largest part of the money used for the research conducted at Wiley Labs. Petrocelli shook his head. "I didn't get it. I guess it's true what they say."

Quade didn't follow him. "What is?"

"When one door shuts another one opens up." Petrocelli blew out a breath that seemed to have the weight of the world attached to it. "I can't tell you how gratified I am that you did this."

"I didn't actually do anything."

Petrocelli waved away the protest. "Modest, brilliant and good-looking. You must be beating them off with a stick, Doctor."

If he hadn't felt uncomfortable before, this would have done it. Whether work-related or personal, Quade hated having attention drawn to him. He preferred moving in and out of things like smoke.

"Most of my time is spent at work. There's no one to beat off," he said, hoping that would be the end of it. Digging into his lab coat, he pulled out one of the cards that MacKenzie had given him. "That's MacKenzie's number. She can put you in touch with Dakota Delaney, or whoever is going to be orchestrating this thing."

Rising, Petrocelli took the card, his fingers closing around it as if it were a good-luck talisman. "Wonderful. Wonderful." His wide, round face wreathed in a smile, he shook Quade's hand. "And when all the details are finalized, I'll get back to you. I want you to deliver the keynote speech."

The salvo came out of nowhere, torpedoing the nascent good feeling that was beginning to nestle into Quade's system. "Excuse me?"

"You came with an incredible long list of accolades from your previous employer. Who better to tell the people with the deep pockets what we're doing here?"

Quade could come up with an entire fleet of people better suited to delivering a speech, up to and probably including the janitor. The thought of standing up in front of a room full of people and speaking threatened to erode the lining of his stomach.

He settled for the most logical protest. "But I've only been here a week."

"You've been working at finding a cure for leukemia a great deal longer than a week, Doctor. Besides, they'll want to hear from someone who's in the trenches, not someone who got his degree in glad-handing." The smile Petrocelli gave him was meant to encourage Quade. "Trust me, your type is in."

This was what he got for becoming involved, Quade thought. The sidelines were looking better and better. At least he couldn't make a fool of himself from there. "Type?"

"Modest, brilliant and good-looking," Petrocelli re-iterated. "If I had a daughter your age, I'd be bringing her in to meet you." He looked at the card in his hand as if it were a miracle that had materialized on call. "God, I can't thank you enough."

"Not necessary," Quade muttered under his breath. Damn, how had he gotten himself tangled up like this? All he'd intended to do was be a messenger, a go-between. How had he gotten caught in the middle?

The intercom buzzed. The secretary's voice followed a beat later, reminding Petrocelli of his first meeting.

"On my way, Hannah," he told her, then looked at Quade. "I'll get back to you," he promised.

Shell-shocked, Quade could only say, "Right," as he left the room. He was vaguely aware that Petrocelli had uttered another "thank you" in his wake.

If the man really wanted to thank him, he'd pass the responsibility of making a speech to someone else. Some-one whose tongue didn't suddenly feel as if it weighed ten pounds at the mere thought of delivering a speech.

He made his way out, oblivious to the secretary he passed.

That was twice in three days that he'd felt as if he'd ventured out into a minefield without realizing it, Quade thought. Kissing MacKenzie might be momentarily more pleasurable than giving a speech, but both were equally unnerving to him. Both guaranteed to make his system go haywire.

Having lost what little of his appetite he'd had, Quade skipped lunch and went back to the lab. Hoping work would get his mind off everything.

* * *

It didn't.

Work only managed to reinforce what was on Quade's mind.

He'd done his part, passed along MacKenzie's number and Dakota Delaney's offer to Petrocelli. Technically he was out of it—except for the speech he'd gotten roped into giving. But even that might be gotten around, he thought. At least it was worth a try.

What he couldn't get around was that he owed MacKenzie a call. After what she'd done it was only polite to fill in his neighbor on Petrocelli's reaction.

Stripping off the latex gloves he'd been wearing, Quade moved back from the table and dipped his hand into his pocket. The other business card MacKenzie had given him was still there. Taking it out, he pressed the numbers that connected him to her cell phone.

She answered on the second ring, sounding a little breathless. A whole series of questions popped up in his head. He banked them down and launched into the reason behind his call.

"I gave your card to Adam Petrocelli. He's the chief financial officer for Wiley Memorial."

The sound of his voice warmed MacKenzie. She wondered if he realized that he hadn't identified himself or even bothered to say hello. MacKenzie smiled to herself. The man was an original.

"I know. He already called. Sounds very excited." She heard what sounded like a suppressed sigh on the other end of the line. She would have thought that Quade would be happy about this. "Something wrong?"

He was about to say no. It wasn't as if he were even remotely accustomed to sharing his feelings about things, especially things that bothered him. But in a way, he supposed she was involved in this.

"Petrocelli wants me to give the keynote speech at the fund-raiser."

"Excellent."

He could almost hear her beaming. The woman probably gave speeches in her sleep.

"Not so excellent," he told her. "I don't know the first thing about giving a speech, keynote or otherwise." If he had anything noteworthy to say about the research he was doing, he put it in writing to share with other researchers. He'd never once gotten up in front of a group to talk about the small headway he was making or about the numerous setbacks he'd endured.

"But you know about your work, don't you? Just talk about that," MacKenzie suggested.

She heard a small, dry laugh. The sound rippled along her skin. She pressed the receiver closer to her ear.

"And put everyone to sleep?"

"It won't be as bad as all that," she assured him. She'd never met anyone as self-effacing as Quade was. "Tell you what—you can practice on me if you like. And maybe I can help you keep the speech from turning into the next big cure for insomnia," she teased. She hesitated for a moment, not wanting to throw another wrench into the works, especially since he'd been the one to call her, but she might as well make the arrangements now. If she didn't, she'd only have to seek him out later. "By the way, Dakota would like to meet you."

For a man whose chief goal in life was to be left in peace, he was certainly drawing an incredible amount of fire. "Excuse me?"

"Dakota's always been a people person and she likes meeting the people who are involved in a cause when she gives her name to it."

He could understand that. What he didn't understand was what the star of *...And Now a Word from Dakota* wanted with him. Other than drawing a salary for his work, he hardly figured into this. "Isn't she meeting with Petrocelli?"

"Yes, but you're the one who first brought this to light."

Quade paused. He tried to remember how all of this had originally unfolded. "I mentioned it to you over dinner. I was just making conversation and nothing else came to mind." And let this be a lesson to him, he thought. From now on, he was going to limit his conversations to simple one-word answers, nothing more.

"You can tell her all that when you meet her," MacKenzie told him cheerfully. "It'll just be for a few minutes," she assured him. "Relax, I've never known Dakota to bite." She laughed and he tried to block the sound, but it was too late. It worked its way into his system, unearthing the same response he'd had to her the other day. When he'd kissed her. "And even if she did, I'm sure you've got something down at Wiley Memorial that covers that."

He sighed. He didn't have to be a war veteran to know when he was outflanked. Quade had no doubt that MacKenzie would go on talking until he surrendered.

"There's no way out of this, is there?" Even as he asked, he already knew the answer.

"Well, she's not the Queen of England—she can't command you to come, but it would be a nice thing if you did."

He wasn't interested in being nice, just in being left alone. But even he knew that you got more things with honey than you did with vinegar and, right now, Wiley Memorial needed all the honey it could find.

Still, he felt it was only fair to warn the woman who had put herself out on a limb for him. "You said she was a people person. I'm not. I'm a loner. I do best when I'm left alone."

"Later," MacKenzie promised, "when this fund-raiser is behind you and Wiley Memorial is back on its way to thriving, you can go back to being a loner. Right now, I'm afraid that your company needs you," she quipped.

MacKenzie was right. Much as he didn't want to, Quade had no choice but to agree with her. "So when do you want to set up the meeting?"

"As soon as possible. Petrocelli is coming by on Wednesday. Why don't you come by the set tomorrow? One o'clock's a good time."

"Why don't I just come with Petrocelli?" he asked. That way, he wouldn't have to say too much. Petrocelli was the kind of man who took over a room whenever he entered. It wasn't in his nature not to.

"Because she wants to meet you first."

"Why?"

"Who knows?" she lied.

She knew exactly why Dakota wanted to meet him separately. It had to do with the damn cameo. Dakota was convinced it held some kind of magical power and she was fixating on the fact that Quade had turned up a day after MacKenzie had begun wearing the necklace.

But since Dakota was going out of her way to arrange for the fund-raiser, the least MacKenzie could do was go along with this.

However, saying any of this to Quade was a guarantee that the man would head for the nearest mountain range and hide there.

"Who knows" was definitely the safer route to go.

MacKenzie was right, Quade thought, walking out of Dakota Delaney's dressing room the following day. The hostess was a vivacious, outgoing woman who didn't seem jaded by either her fame or her lavish upbringing.

The meeting MacKenzie had arranged had lasted twenty minutes. Twenty minutes that were filled with hot- and cold-running people, an endless stream of interruptions and dozens of last-minute details that had to be attended to before Dakota went on the air that afternoon. With MacKenzie at her side, the woman multitasked and never missed a beat of the conversation between them.

His own head was spinning.

It was utter and total chaos within the small room and he had no idea how either Dakota or MacKenzie functioned. To his surprise, and despite his efforts to remain polite but distant, he'd found himself liking the woman.

And liking MacKenzie even more.

The latter really troubled him.

Her ever-present clipboard in her hand, MacKenzie

was quick to follow Quade out into the hallway after the short interview was over.

She beamed as she caught up to him. "Didn't I tell you she was great?"

He nodded. It wasn't in him to voice the kind of enthusiastic rhetoric the way she did. "For someone in the TV industry, she's very nice." And then he paused, unable to repress the question any longer. "How do you stand it?"

"What, Dakota being nice? I put up with it as best I can," MacKenzie deadpanned.

"No, working in that kind of environment." He jerked a thumb back at the dressing room to get his meaning across. A tall, thin makeup artist was just rushing into the room Quade had vacated moments ago. "I couldn't hear myself think."

She shrugged. "Fortunately, I seem to be able to think louder than you do. Silence makes me edgy."

He looked at her a long moment. "I guess we're really opposites."

"I guess so," she agreed. And they seemed to be. In so many different ways.

So why do I want to kiss you again so much? he wondered. *Why do I want you to kiss me? And why the hell does my brain feel like scrambled eggs every time I'm around you?*

"I'd better get back to the lab," Quade murmured.

She nodded. There were places she had to be, as well, instead of here, basking in the shadow he cast. "I'll be in touch."

"I'm sure you will be," he said, turning on his heel.

The fact that she would be invading his life again and soon didn't bother Quade nearly as much as he thought it should.

Which bothered him.

Chapter Ten

Stumbling through the maze of small tables scattered about the floor of the dimly lit club known as the Laugh-Inn, Quade lowered his head and growled against MacKenzie's ear, "Haven't they paid their electricity bill?"

She tried not to let the feel of his breath along her skin scramble her synapses any more than they already were. His warm breath, which was raising goose bumps along her flesh, was nothing more than exhaled air from a fellow mammal.

It didn't help.

Perhaps because she'd been kissed by this particular mammal, or because the man looked like the dream fantasy of every woman with a pulse. Package that dream fantasy with considerable brain power and you had the perfect male.

Almost.

What kept Quade from attaining the title of perfect male, in her estimation, was his brooding manner. Granted, a great many women out there wanted to experience life with James Dean. They were the same ones who loved the idea of having a "bad boy" they could try to reform, but she wasn't among them. Bad boys belonged in corners, facing the wall, not as one's life partner.

Not that she was contemplating getting a partner, she reminded herself as she stepped around a table occupied by a couple kissing each other into oblivion. At this point in her life, she just wanted to get through her day without any major mishaps and then crash into bed at night.

This evening's crash had been temporarily postponed because she and Quade had been commandeered to lend moral support to Aggie.

As good as her word, Aggie was trying out her newly synthesized "act" at the Laugh-Inn. The woman had lain in wait for each of them last night, springing out the moment they'd separately emerged from their cars. She'd tendered a verbal invitation along with a plea to come and cheer her on tonight.

It was hard turning down someone who looked like your grandmother in need, MacKenzie thought. But if anyone could have turned Aggie down, she figured Quade would be the one to do it. Yet here he was. Scowling, but here.

He'd even gone so far as to offer to drive. She'd accepted without even thinking about it.

She drew in her breath as she felt his hand against

her back, guiding her. Warmth flooded her. When had they cut off the air to the place?

MacKenzie forced herself to focus on the question he'd growled and not on the effect he was having on her. "I think it's because they don't want you to notice that the walls need painting and the tables could stand a restaining."

Now, rather than walking behind her, he was next to her. And giving her that look that could have easily X-rayed her entire body. "You noticed."

She shrugged. "It's the domestic side of me."

She had almost made a comment about a nesting instinct taking over, but stopped herself just in time. It was the kind of comment that would immediately send a man running for the hills, eager to put miles between himself and the female who uttered it.

But the urge for nesting had nothing to do with him and everything to do with the baby inside of her.

"This table okay?" the waitress who had been leading the way asked. She didn't bother to wait for a reply, but abruptly walked away in response to someone gesturing for her at a nearby table.

"I guess she really didn't want an answer to that," MacKenzie commented. About to sit down, she was surprised when Quade pulled out the chair for her, then helped her in. "Thank you," she murmured.

Quade slid into his own chair and faced the stage. "Don't look so surprised. I wasn't about to pull it out from under you."

"I know that—it's just that chivalry is so rare these days."

"Maybe it shouldn't be," he said gruffly, looking around as his eyes grew accustomed to his surroundings.

The dimly lit room had approximately fifteen tables in it, most for two, some for three and one long one that accommodated eight in the rear of the small room. Seven people were spread out around it now. Obviously the family and/or friends of one of the performers risking mental castration tonight, Quade thought darkly. He settled in, prepared to make the best of it. Hoping it wouldn't last too long.

MacKenzie had come reluctantly. Not because she didn't want to be supportive, but because she hated that queasy, unsettled feeling that came over her by proxy. The one she was sure was shared by police personnel assigned to the bomb squad. She'd been in the entertainment business for more than a handful of years now and yet, each time she was privy to a performer's debut, she felt as if she were channeling their nervousness through her own body. Her palms grew sweaty.

There were times when her ability to empathize really was challenging.

Quade brushed against her hand as he reached for the single-paged, slightly stained menu in front of the candle. Surprised, he looked at her. If anything, the club was overly warm. "Your hands as cold as ice."

"Nerves."

"Why? You're not going on."

"I know. I just get nervous for performers," she confessed. "Especially if I know them."

"You didn't have to come," he pointed out matter-of-factly. Nothing on the menu moved him. He set it down again.

She wondered if things were always completely black-and-white in his world. She would have liked to think not. "Nothing worse than going on without a friendly face in the audience."

It still made no sense to him. "I would have been here."

"Well, I couldn't have been sure of that and, besides, I wouldn't exactly call your face friendly." She touched it before she could think out her action. A zap of electricity telegraphed itself to her. More nerves, but of a different variety. She needed a long vacation, she decided. Alone. "At least," MacKenzie amended, not wanting to insult him, "not most of the time."

The waitress appeared before Quade answered her. With one hip jutting up higher than the other, the young woman's stance was expectant as she looked from MacKenzie's face to Quade's.

"So? What'll it be?" Her tone told them to make it snappy, that she had better things to do than stand in front of a table, waiting for the occupants' order. "There's a two-drink minimum."

Out of habit, MacKenzie began to order a white wine. She stopped herself at the last moment. Although her mother's generation had never had the no-alcohol rule and had produced healthy babies, she was not about to take any chances on her future child's welfare. Besides, she had already given up her life-affirming cup of coffee in the morning. Giving up alcohol for the next eight months was far less of a challenge.

"I'll have a ginger ale," she told the waitress.

The brassy blonde tugged on one of the three earrings she wore in her right earlobe and stared at MacKenzie as if she were some kind of freak of nature. "You one of those Pennsylvania Dutch type people?"

A note of annoyance entered MacKenzie's voice. She was hot, tired and nervous. She didn't need attitude. "No, I'm not Amish. I just like ginger ale."

"Make that two," Quade said, drawing the woman's scornful look away from MacKenzie.

"You want a ginger ale, too?"

"That's what I said." His voice was low, steely and not to be trifled with.

Shrugging, the waitress tugged back the neckline that had slipped off her shoulder and then sauntered away. "Customer's always right," she muttered in a tone that said she believed just the opposite.

Why Quade's simple gestured affected MacKenzie so, she couldn't say. There was a warmth in the center of her belly that hadn't been there before. She leaned in toward him in order to be heard above the din. "You didn't have to do that."

Gratitude slid off him like rain down a windowpane. He preferred being without it. "I didn't like her condescending attitude. You've got a right to order anything you want."

Still, she had a feeling he would have preferred something stronger, at least a beer. All the men she'd ever known had preferred beer to soft drinks. "Do you even like ginger ale?"

He shrugged away the question. "I didn't come here because I needed to drink."

That part of his life was behind him. There were no answers in the bottom of a bottle. He'd learned that the hard way after he'd almost drowned in one. He had no desire to return to the scene of the crime. It took more courage facing life sober and he'd never liked thinking of himself as a coward.

"I came here because Aggie asked me to come," he told MacKenzie. "Since there's a two-drink minimum, I have to order. But there's no rule that says I have to order what a waitress with the upbringing of a disaffected orangutan thinks I should order."

MacKenzie was grinning at him. And her smile did a great deal more to light up the place than the meager floating candles in the center of each table. He had to mentally pull back before he was completely drawn in to the woman.

"What?"

"That's probably the most you've said at one time since I've met you."

"It probably is," he agreed.

The waitress returned with their ginger ales. She disdainfully placed a glass in front of each of them, then sullenly withdrew as someone else called to get her attention.

"Keep your shirt on—they don't pay me to hurry," she barked.

They obviously didn't pay her to be polite, either, MacKenzie thought. She took a sip and then looked at Quade. "Think Aggie will be any good?"

His mind immediately turned toward Aggie. "God, I hope so."

It would be hard enough to sit through this if the woman was good. If she was bad, it would be utter torture. Especially if she asked his opinion. He'd never been able to lie, even under the best of circumstances. The only time he'd actually tried was to tell Ellen she was going to get well.

He looked so solemn for a moment, MacKenzie strove to change the subject. "Dakota got in contact with Mr. Petrocelli."

She saw mild interest enter his eyes as he watched her. The atmosphere within the club smelled faintly of cheap liquor and the scent of fear emanating from the people clustered just off stage right, waiting to come out and meet either life-affirming laughter or soul-robbing silence. None of this could seem even remotely romantic and yet, with the small candles flickering on each table and the low murmur of voices in the background, that was exactly what it was to her. Romantic.

Or maybe it had to do with the man sitting opposite her at a table hardly large enough for two. With every movement, every shift on her seat, she felt her leg brush against his. Felt something akin to a current passing through her, putting her on notice. Making her alert.

She had a hard time concentrating on where she was, on who she was. It had to be the pregnancy that made her feel strongly toward him. And yet, a small part of her rejoiced over her reaction to Quade. Rejoiced because a very large part of her had thought that after her breakup with Jeff, she had ceased to feel anything at all. And that had made her very afraid. She took another drink of her ginger ale. How had life gotten so very complicated?

She realized that Quade was waiting for her to follow up the statement that now seemed to be flapping madly in the wind, unaccompanied by more words.

"And?" he finally prodded.

"They agreed on a date. She's free for an evening the night of the twenty-eighth. It's a Saturday," she added in case he didn't know.

Quade felt like a man who had just been led into a windowless room and had the door slam shut behind him. "That's in two and a half weeks."

"Too soon?" she guessed. It wasn't really a guess. She'd seen stage fright before, even when it was as well masked as this. There was a slight flare to his sculpted nose, a discomfort around the eyes.

He leveled with her, although he didn't ordinarily share his thoughts with people. "To find a tux, no. To write a speech, yes."

She placed her hand over his in silent camaraderie. "You'll do a great job."

She sounded a hell of a lot more confident about it than he did. He knew better but was reasonably sure that to say so would only pull him into a lengthy discussion, one which he knew he hadn't a prayer of winning.

For one thing, her mouth moved a great deal faster than his did.

He didn't even bother making the attempt.

The next moment, a haggard-looking man came out and crossed to the lone microphone standing forlornly in the center of the stage.

A small drumroll accompanied him and a guitarist, the owner's son, sat to the right of the man's drum set.

The drumroll effectively sliced through the residual conversation until silence eventually followed.

MacKenzie doubted she'd ever seen a more forced smile than the one beneath the emcee's rather matted mustache.

"Hi, I'm Henderson Ames, the emcee and the owner of the club. Most of you know me as Henny." Not a single murmur greeted the statement. "I see a lot of faces I recognize and a few new ones."

The owner seemed to be looking in their direction, but MacKenzie couldn't be sure. Their table was two rows back from the front and Ames was cut off by the glare of a single, lonely spotlight.

"You all know the drill by now. We've got a handful of would-be comics, some repeaters. They'll all compete against each other. If you think that the next Robin Williams or Whoopi Goldberg is among them, show me by your applause. The winner gets the handsome prize of fifty bucks." Someone in the audience groaned. "Hey, it buys a meal or two. Am I right?" He beckoned for an answer and there were murmurs of agreement. The man smiled broadly again, reminding MacKenzie of a snake in a fabled children's movie. "So, without any further delay, let's bring out our first performer. Stoker Michaels."

He backed away as the man he had just introduced took the stage. MacKenzie noticed that the latter's hand trembled ever so slightly as he took hold of the microphone.

She could feel her stomach pitching.

Aggie was the fourth on the bill. By the time the

older woman came out, MacKenzie had felt mortified twice and laughed three times at the second performer. The man had walked off, beaming as if he felt he owned the evening.

A slight murmur rippled through the crowd. It was obvious that no one had expected anyone over the age of thirty to be starting out on a career as a stand-up comedian.

Aggie came out wearing a flattering navy-blue tunic and matching pants. Taking the microphone in hand, she looked as comfortable with it as she had handling a spatula over the stove in her apartment the other night.

Quade thought of the speech he was going to have to deliver and envied the woman her apparent ease.

For a moment, after the welcoming applause had died down, coming most zealously from MacKenzie, there was nothing but silence.

MacKenzie held her breath. She was afraid that Aggie had forgotten the beginning of her act or, worse, had become frozen with stage fright.

The next minute, she realized that she could have saved herself the agony by proxy. Aggie was just searching the crowd for a target to focus on in order to begin her act.

Finally, she zeroed in on a bald man sitting beside a petite woman. "You there. The man with the pretty lady sitting at his side. Yes, you," she affirmed when the bald man pointed to himself. "You have a mother-in-law? Of course you do," she said quickly before he could respond. "Your face looks as if you've been drinking persimmon juice for an hour. Always a sure sign." Moving away from the man, she focused on the rest of the audience, treating them as if they had all melded into one person, a confidante she was about to unload on. "Everyone who's married has a mother-in-law, unless they're lucky enough to have married an orphan." She smiled broadly, wistfully. "That's what I told my kids— marry an orphan. Or I'm not coming to the wedding. Think I'm not serious? I'm deadly serious. I didn't want them to go through what I did."

She paused, waiting for the words to sink in. Aggie made MacKenzie think of a mischievous pixie.

"Oh, I know what you're thinking. She's older than dirt. Did they even *have* mothers-in-law when she got married? Let me tell you, they did and the one I got moonlights as a stand-in for Satan."

She rolled her eyes, sighing dramatically as she worked the stage from one end to the other. "Just about drove me crazy. My mother-in-law, or, Stupid Woman—as she was known by her Native American name—was so dumb—" another dramatic pause before she went on to elaborate "—I've known buttons to have higher IQs. But that didn't stop her from knowing how to manipulate."

Aggie continued in the same vein for the ten minutes that had been allotted to her, gathering momentum and laughter as she went.

When she finished her set, the applause was full-bodied and enthusiastic. And no one clapped harder or more enthusiastically than MacKenzie. She clapped so hard, their small table actually shook from the vibrations.

She kept on applauding even after Aggie had left the stage. Finally, Quade placed his hand between hers, abruptly stopping her.

MacKenzie looked at him questioningly.

He nodded at her hands, withdrawing his slowly. "You might find you want to save them for something else," he advised.

Smiling sheepishly at him, she dropped her hands to her lap.

But she felt exhilarated for the older woman. She'd been so afraid that Aggie was going to fall flat on her face. MacKenzie had seen what disappointment did to people. No matter what a performer said about being tough and being able to handle criticism, they were all just children at heart. Children who craved acceptance, validation and praise. Thank God, that was what Aggie had received.

MacKenzie beamed at Quade. "She was good, wasn't she?"

"Yes," he replied patiently, "she was good." He would have thought that was self-evident and didn't need to be pointed out.

MacKenzie exhaled. It seemed to him as if she'd been holding her breath the entire time Aggie had been on. "Can't tell you how relieved I am," she said.

But then, the last contestant came out and she had to leave anything else she was going to add unsaid until later.

After fifteen minutes, Ames returned with all five of that evening's participants.

"And now it's time for what we've all been waiting for. The money." He waited for a polite laugh to clear the air, then continued.

He held his hand over the head of each contestant, urging the audience to chose their favorite for the night.

It wasn't even close.

While each contestant had at least one table applauding for him or her, the applause went from forced to spirited when it came to Aggie.

"Well, looks like we have ourselves a winner." Ames handed Aggie the money. "And a repeat performer?" he asked.

Aggie beamed, placing the single bill into her pocket. "Just try and stop me."

"Such zest, such enthusiasm." He winked broadly at the audience. "If I were just fifteen years older—"

"You'd be dead," Aggie quipped.

Stunned, the man laughed and, for once, the sound didn't seem forced. "Give it up for Aggie. You saw her first here at the Laugh-Inn."

"You were wonderful," MacKenzie declared as the woman came to join them several minutes later. She threw her arms around Aggie in a quick embrace before allowing her to join them at the table.

Aggie's expression was fond as the she looked at MacKenzie. "You would have said that if I was struck dumb and fell on my face." She turned her attention to Quade. "How about you, handsome? Did I make you laugh out loud or does the act need work?"

Quade inclined his head. "It was very good," he told her in all honesty.

"I know what that means." Aggie took her pad out of her pants pocket. "Act needs work," she said aloud and wrote down. She then tucked the pad away again with a broad wink toward MacKenzie and rose to her feet. "C'mon, let's blow this Popsicle stand. I've got fifty dollars burning a hole in my pocket and I want to feed my support group."

Quade glanced at his watch and then at MacKenzie. The younger woman looked rather tired in his opinion. "It's kind of late, Aggie."

"Only in England," she declared, slipping her arm through his and urging him toward the door. She beckoned for MacKenzie to keep up.

There was no arguing with her.

Chapter Eleven

There was a tiny Chinese restaurant just two blocks from the club. Located between a florist and a shoe-repair shop, it was often overlooked. Which made it, according to Aggie, a secret piece of heaven.

The food certainly was worth the extra effort in finding it. The ambiance was more on a par with eating in someone's kitchen than a restaurant. But that gave Mandarin Rose the extra attraction of treating its patrons like family.

Distant family, MacKenzie noted, because there was somewhat of a language barrier. But that was overcome with gestures and pointing to things on the red-rimmed, worn, gold-lettered menu.

By the time the fortune cookies arrived, MacKenzie felt as if she were going to explode. She dubiously eyed the small plate with its three fortune cookies. She sincerely doubted that there was enough room inside of her to consume even that tiny amount of sugar and dough.

"Ever notice that when the three of us get together, we wind up eating?" she commented as Aggie placed her newly acquired fifty on top of the bill.

The older woman's hand went up like a policewoman stopping traffic. "Wait, there's a joke in there somewhere." As the lone waitress withdrew with the tray, Aggie whipped out her pad and began to scribble the words down.

"No," MacKenzie countered, "there are calories in there everywhere and I need to watch what I eat. I'm just five foot three and I can balloon up in the blink of an eye." She glanced down at her waist. While she still could, she thought ruefully. "I can't afford to gain any more weight."

With a laugh, Aggie tucked her pad back in her purse. Her brilliant blue eyes slid to the side, taking in the all-but-silent member of their party. "What do you think, Quade? Think she's in danger of being too heavy?"

Quade shrugged as if he hadn't been giving the matter any thought. As if he hadn't been subconsciously studying MacKenzie's trim, athletic body every time she approached or was near him. "She's fine just as she is."

The simple, offhanded comment surprised MacKenzie. More than that, it warmed her. She came from a world where compliments were as common as leaves on a tree. They were far too plentiful and usually far too empty. But Quade was incredibly sparing in his comments and a kind observation, well, that was just about worth its weight in gold.

MacKenzie hugged the words to her, even as she silently upbraided herself for being so adolescent.

But she did it anyway.

"Go on, choose your fortune," Aggie urged, gesturing to the plate that still remained on the table.

After a beat, MacKenzie selected one. She cracked it open and extracted the small rectangular wisp of paper.

"Well, what does it say?" Aggie urged.

"Love will find you." She crumpled it up and tossed it back onto the plate. She wondered if Dakota was back in the small kitchen, stuffing fortune cookies. "Very original."

"Doesn't have to be original," Aggie pointed out, opening her own. "It just has to be."

MacKenzie had given up on that concept. If love existed, it was entirely out of her realm. "What's yours say?"

"Success is within your reach." Aggie's eyes gleamed. "I like the sound of that." And then she looked at Quade. "Your turn, Quade."

He picked up the remaining one and broke it open with his thumb and forefinger. And then he laughed shortly, dropping it back onto the plate.

"Doesn't look as if there's much originality in the fortune cookie business."

Curious, MacKenzie picked up the fortune he'd discarded and read, "Love will find you." Same as hers. Now she really was tempted to see if Dakota had sneaked into the back. She placed his fortune beside her own. "You're right. They need a new writer."

A smug smile curved the edges of Aggie's mouth as she looked from one dinner companion to the next. She said nothing.

MacKenzie felt the nesting instinct taking hold of her a good six months earlier than it should have. From what she'd heard, women in their ninth month were suddenly seized with the desire to straighten, to clean. To put rooms, if not life itself, in order.

It didn't usually hit a woman in the beginning of her third month. But then, women didn't usually get pregnant when they were on birth-control pills. She figured that put her in a class all by herself.

Any spare moment she had that didn't directly involve her job was spent being incredibly domestic. Her own apartment was quickly rendered spotless, as was her office. Needing to find an outlet for the charged energy she suddenly possessed now that her fatigue had mysteriously evaporated, MacKenzie had moved on to taming the chaotic state of Dakota's dressing room. She would have gone on to tidy up the station's program director's suite had she been allowed inside.

With nothing left for her to organize, catalog or clean, MacKenzie turned her attention toward things culinary.

As with everything else she did, she went a little overboard.

Her latest attack had struck after she'd come home from work Friday afternoon with bulging grocery bags. The ingredients for oatmeal cookies were on the bottom. She threw herself into the venture and wound up baking enough cookies to satisfy a murder of scavenging crows.

And if she didn't get rid of at least some of them, she thought, looking critically at the grand outcome, odds were she was going to turn into the Goodyear blimp by Monday morning.

Aggie wasn't in when MacKenzie knocked on the woman's door. With a sigh, she took her offering to Quade's apartment. A glance toward his parking space told her that he was in. Or at least, that his car had been left in its place. She knew that some mornings he opted to catch the bus rather than fight traffic.

She rang his bell, thinking she'd probably get the same response she'd gotten at Aggie's. Loneliness sprang up out of nowhere even before her hand left the doorbell.

When the door opened, MacKenzie was more surprised to see him than he was to see her.

Quade eyed the enormous pile of oatmeal cookies. It was precariously held in place with clear plastic wrap. One wrong move, he judged, and it was all going to land on the floor.

"Knock over a group of Girl Scouts?"

Quade opened his door wider. At this point, he knew better than to expect her to leave if he just held the door ajar long enough. He'd come to learn MacKenzie Ryan was like smoke. She always found a way to infiltrate his space. He figured there was no point in fighting the matter. He might as well save his energy and use it where it counted.

He found the rueful flush that raced across her cheeks captivating. "No, I just got carried away baking."

Closing the door behind her, he shook his head. "You do that a lot, don't you?"

She turned, looking at him over her shoulder. "Bake? No, I just—"

His laugh cut her short. "No, I meant get carried away."

She lifted one shoulder in a half shrug. "Sometimes," she allowed.

Most times, she added silently. She set down the teeming plate on the coffee table and then looked around for the first time since she'd walked in. Not a single box had been cleared away or even opened since she'd last been there.

She turned to glance at him. Her palms began to itch. "You haven't unpacked yet."

He looked at the tall, sealed cartons as if they comprised the enemy. And, in a way, they did. They held his past in them. A past in which he'd been happy, but that hurt too much to revisit. He was working on constructing barriers strong enough to withstand the assault.

"I'll get to it."

"Thinking of leaving?" she guessed.

MacKenzie realized that she didn't like the taste of the words she uttered. It force her to admit that she liked having Quade next door, liked looking to see if his car was parked in his spot when she arrived home each day.

Liked anticipating the possibility of running into him.

His tone was dismissive, meant to call an end to any further discussion of the subject. "No, I just don't like to unpack, that's all."

She turned toward the closest box, taking hold of the

edge of the masking tape. Her nesting instinct had gone into high gear at the sight of the boxes. There was no reason not to help him unpack. It would be doing them both a favor.

"Well, if that's all—" she gave the tape a tug and it began to come loose "—I'm pretty good at—"

"No." It was an order, not a request, sharply given. He crossed to her and put his hand on top of hers, stopping her from ripping the tape completely off. "Leave that alone."

She looked at him, uncertain at what had set him off like that. She certainly hadn't intended on sounding as if she were being disrespectful. Still, she thought he'd just gone off the deep end there.

"I wasn't going to sell it on eBay. I was just trying to help," she told him. "My mother used to hate to unpack groceries when she came home from the store, so I always did it."

The woman really did have an answer for everything, he thought darkly. "These aren't groceries."

"No, they're not." She stood by the box, waiting him out. No man liked to unpack. "I could still figure out where the contents went if you gave me a general hint."

He blew out a breath, dragging his hand through his hair. Damn, he'd overreacted. But it was hard not to. Every time he thought the wound was healing, the scab felt as if it were being pulled off again and he went back to square one.

He pressed his lips together. "Look, I'm sorry. I didn't mean to snap at you like that."

MacKenzie's hand flew up to her chest as she looked

at him in mock, wide-eyed wonder. "Wow, first a compliment the other night, now an apology, I should circle this week on my calendar."

He scowled at her. "I'm not exactly good with people."

"All the more reason to circle the week," she told him cheerfully. "You're a lot more communicative now than when I first met you. You're making progress, Quade." She patted his cheek. There was just the barest hint of a five o'clock shadow moving across it. Something warm and excited rippled through her before she could prevent it. "Baby steps."

He didn't want to be making any progress, baby steps or otherwise.

What he wanted was to be left alone, but no one was listening.

Still, he supposed it wasn't MacKenzie's fault. In that scrambled head of hers, she was trying to do what she thought was right.

"Whatever," he murmured.

She unwrapped the plate she'd brought, picked up the top cookie and held it out to him. "Here, have a cookie." When he took it almost grudgingly, she added, "And let me help."

He could only shake his head. "You don't give up, do you?"

The expression in her eyes was earnest, despite the smile on her lips. "Never get anywhere by giving up."

It sounded like a slogan someone should have sewn on some kind of a banner. Absently, he took a bite out of the cookie she'd given him and felt an explosion of taste on his tongue. Sweet, tantalizing.

Like she had been when he'd kissed her.

Needs moved forward within him like an army making its way toward the line of battle.

He frowned as he looked from the cartons back to her. She seemed so damn eager, you'd think she was a child, looking for a prize inside of a Cracker Jack box. "If I let you do one box, will that satisfy you?"

She began to protest that she wasn't doing it out of some need that had to be satisfied, but then realized that, in a way, she was. His boxes had become her challenge. She meant either to unpack them or have him do it himself. Either way, the cardboard had to go.

"It would be a start," she allowed slowly.

He should have found that suspect, but he didn't. Muttering something unintelligible under his breath, he gestured toward the collection of boxes with barely suppressed exasperation.

"All right, pick one."

With a small laugh of triumph, MacKenzie chose the one she'd already begun. When she ripped off the tape, she parted the flaps and took out the first thing that had been packed on top. A framed photograph from the feel of it.

Taking off the tissue paper that had been wrapped tightly around it, she paused to look at the smiling blonde in the photograph. Sister? Girlfriend? More?

"Quade?"

His mouth full of his second cookie, he could only emit a sound. "Mmm?"

Holding the photograph up, she turned it so that he could see. "Who is this?"

She saw the tint of Quade's skin fade into shades of gray.

It felt as if there were lead inside of his chest instead of a heart that was supposed to keep him functioning. He put down the box he'd just picked up and strode across the room.

"My wife," he told her, taking the frame out of her hands.

MacKenzie felt as if someone had punched her. The intensity she experienced was a rude awakening to just how much she'd allowed herself to be drawn to him in an incredibly short period of time.

His answer was her cue to go. To quietly bow out, leave him to his boxes, his memories and his thoughts and look to her own survival. She was pregnant, about to begin one hell of a new adventure in her life. This was *not* a time to fall for another man.

Especially not a married one.

Been there, done that.

But for some unfathomable reason, she couldn't make herself leave. "Are you separated?" she heard herself asking, damning the hope inside of her. That was what Jeff had told her he was before he'd gone back to his wife. He was separated. Not separated enough.

"Yes," Quade replied, his voice hollow and echoing in his head. "Permanently."

The solemnity of his tone threw her. Was he still carrying a torch for the woman? Was that why there was such sorrow in his eyes? "You're divorced?"

Funny, it took courage to say it, even after all this time. Courage because the word sliced him into a hundred pieces. "No, widowed, actually. She died eighteen months ago."

Envy, jealousy and fledgling anger all vanished into thin air. Sympathy flooded the space they left behind. "Oh, Quade, I'm so sorry."

But even as she uttered the words, there was a small trickle of relief flowing through her. Relief that had nothing to do with the fact that he was widowed or technically available, and everything to do with the fact that once he had loved a woman enough to want to make her his exclusively.

It made him human. And as vulnerable as she felt.

The soft, disparaging laugh caught her attention. She looked at him, curious.

His eyes met hers, but he couldn't believe that he was opening up to her. "Want to hear the ironic part? Ellen died of leukemia. The exact disease I was oh-so-busy trying to find a cure for." His voice mocked his efforts. There were times he felt that it was all rather futile. Like a dog chasing its own tail.

He raised his eyes to look at her again. "Quite a kick in the pants, don't you think?"

She wanted to hug him, to hold him. To tell him how sorry she was that he had been hurt. That he *was* hurting. She could almost feel his pain, could feel the loneliness undulating through her.

It wasn't all that different from the loneliness she felt herself. "I don't know what to think."

He looked at her in surprise. His mouth curved slightly. "Well, that's a first."

MacKenzie knew what he was doing, trying to divert

her attention. She wouldn't allow herself to get side-tracked. "It hurts, doesn't it?" she murmured. "Losing someone."

"Damn straight it does." Something in MacKenzie's voice caught his attention, which was a first for him, he supposed. He normally wasn't in tune to other people's feelings.

"Did you lose someone?" he asked.

Maybe it would anger him, she thought, having his situation compared to hers. "In a manner of speaking," she replied slowly. "He didn't die. He just went back to the wife I never knew he had, wearing my heart on his sleeve."

"Oh." He tried to think of what he could say by way of comfort, but nothing came to mind. He wasn't any good at this kind of thing. "I'm sorry."

"Yes, so am I," MacKenzie said in a small voice, thinking of the baby she was carrying.

The baby she should have found a way to prevent.

But now that it was a part of her, a child waiting to happen, she couldn't bring herself just to sweep it out of her life, to white it out like a mistake on a page.

But what kind of a life was she going to give it? It was so hard for a child with only one parent. And Jeff was never going to want to be a part of his or her life. That was going to be painful.

She already hurt for the baby she hadn't even held in her arms yet.

Quade saw the tears shimmering in her eyes. Something twisted inside of him, stirring emotions he wanted to keep banked down.

What he wanted didn't seem to matter here.

"You loved him a lot."

It wasn't really a question, but she answered him anyway.

"Yes, I did." Her mouth curved in self-deprecation. "More of that misguided enthusiasm you commented on the other day." That was always her failing, she thought. She moved before her mind caught up to the rest of her. "I just jumped right in with both feet, never noticing the signs."

"Signs?"

"That he still belonged to someone else." It had been three months since they'd broken up, but she still felt the need to deflect blows on Jeff's behalf. How pathetic was that? She couldn't seem to help herself. "In his defense, he was actually separated at the time we met, but he never mentioned that. Told me later that he was afraid I wouldn't go out with him if he did. So he just conveniently tucked that little annoying fact away."

"He should have told you," he agreed.

"Yes, he should have." Then, maybe, she wouldn't be in this position, she thought. Turning away, she started to unpack the carton.

He looked at her back for a long moment. People did incredibly stupid things when they were in love. "Would it have made a difference?"

Taking out a set of books, she paused for a second. Thinking of the baby. "You have no idea."

She made herself get back to what she was doing. Keeping busy was the best remedy for what ailed her. She couldn't help thinking that Quade was being incredibly sweet. Far more sympathetic than she'd ever thought he would be. But then, he'd suffered his own broken heart. It gave them something in common.

For a second, she debated telling him about the baby, but something stopped her. The same thing that had probably stopped Jeff from telling her about his marriage that had been temporarily in limbo. And it wasn't even something she could put into words. She felt a surge of guilt. Nothing good ever came from deception. But she wasn't deceiving, she silently insisted, she was omitting. Technically, there was a difference.

Besides, it wasn't as if the man was having those kinds of thoughts about her. He probably saw her as a nuisance, not someone to care about.

God, she needed someone to care about her.

It took her a second to realize that he had come up from behind and circled around until he was facing her. Tears filled her eyes.

Her damn hormones were acting up again, making her feel sorry for herself. Making her feel things she had no business feeling.

A single tear trickled down her cheek. Oh, great, he was going to think she was some kind of emotionally unstable female, given to crying jags. That wasn't her. She was bright, happy, able to see the upside of everything, even loneliness.

Another tear made good its escape.

She held her breath as he brushed his thumb against her cheek, wiping away the tracks of the tears that spilled out.

"He's not worth crying over."

"I'm not crying over him," she told him quietly. "I guess I'm just mad at myself for being that stupid."

He could feel his heart being tugged one way and then another. After vowing never to feel again, powerful emotions for this woman surged through him. He'd always kept his promises before—why couldn't he keep them now?

"Falling in love isn't stupid," he told her.

She raised her head, forcing a smile to her lips. "Falling for the wrong man is."

"But you had no way of knowing that."

"No." The word spilled in slow motion from her lips. "I didn't."

As they spoke, the small distance between them grew even less. With each word he uttered, his face came closer to hers.

And she found herself raising herself up on her toes, anticipating. Waiting.

Needing.

Reaching up, she framed his face with her hands. "Anyone ever tell you that you were too tall?"

His smile felt warm against her palms as amusement widened it. "Subject never came up."

"Well, you are," she whispered.

"There's a way to remedy that."

The next moment, he raised her in his arms as he simultaneously brought his mouth down to hers.

Chapter Twelve

The kiss grew, swelling until it became everything. Until it pulled them into a vortex of swirling heat and tightly wrapped emotions.

As it deepened, as the sensations claimed them, emotions began to break free of their bonds. It was as if someone had fired a starting pistol at the beginning of a race.

Once committed to the moment, to the action, a frenzy seized them, urging them on to take this unforeseen, precious moment that had crossed their path.

Quade couldn't believe this was happening, couldn't stop himself from being part of it. If MacKenzie had said something, demurred, protested, made him feel that she didn't want this, he would have somehow forced himself to withdraw. To back away even as everything within him begged him to go forward.

But she wasn't pushing him away, wasn't attempting to end the kiss, the moment. If anything, he could taste her acquiescence. Her eagerness.

And that was all he needed to set him on fire.

With urgent hands, Quade swiftly unbuttoned her blouse, his lips never leaving hers.

She echoed his movement, all but tearing the shirt off his chest.

For a split second, he slowed down. Passing his palms ever so lightly against her breasts.

Mentally bracing himself for a termination.

It didn't come.

Instead, he heard her moan. The low, seductive sound raced through his veins like a flash fire, fueling his desire and increasing it tenfold.

He undid the clasp to her bra, got rid of it with no more attention than if it were a barrier constructed of tissue paper.

Her skin felt soft against his. Her flesh warm and smooth and pliant. Quade pressed her to him, the fire growing.

The snug low-rise jeans she wore were next. His fingers brushed against her belly and something in his own tightened sharply, stealing away his air. His belly tightened further as he felt her undoing his belt, felt her fingers on his zipper. Felt her reaching inside for him.

He caught his breath, the fiery kiss between them a five-alarm blaze by now. Air was barely making its way in and out of his lungs.

MacKenzie tugged his trousers off at the same moment that he got rid of her jeans.

She was wearing a thong.

He found that impossibly sexy. His tongue sought out hers as he slowly slid the scrap of material down her hips. Felt the heat and moisture building from her loins. She stepped out of the flimsy garment as he kicked aside his briefs. Shoes had long since disappeared.

They were free.

They were bound.

To one another, the moment and the need that hadn't allowed either of them draw a single unobstructed breath since the moment he'd lowered his mouth to hers.

His body pulsed, vibrating with demands. He wanted to sheath himself inside of her, to feel her softness tighten and close around him.

But then it would be over much too quickly.

And he didn't want it to be over, didn't want the moment, the woman, to turn into something that lived for him only in the past.

He wanted it to continue.

Wanted this wild rush he felt to continue. Because it had been so long that he had been dead inside, so long since he had felt like a man. So long since he had felt alive.

Sweeping her into his arms, still kissing her over and over again, Quade took MacKenzie into his bedroom.

The covers on the bed were all tangled up from the night before. Typical male, he never saw the point in making his bed. The sheets and comforter would only become tangled again by daybreak, so why go through the useless motions?

He wanted to see her in his bed. To make love with her in his bed.

She felt the impression of the mattress against her back as she sank down.

What the hell are you doing? a voice inside her head cried. She'd never, ever gone from zero to a hundred and twenty before, no matter how tempted she'd been to take the ride.

It was as if she'd lost her mind and, in a way, she supposed that she had. Because if she'd still possessed even one ounce of sanity, she wouldn't be here like this with him. Wouldn't have dragged his clothes off his body as if she were some kind of sex-starved, depraved creature out for a thrill.

She wasn't out for *a* thrill, she was out for *the* thrill. With him.

Though she would have never admitted as much to Dakota because the woman was so fixated on the mystical powers of the cameo, there was something about Quade that pressed every single button she possessed. That made her want to abandon what little good sense remained and just give herself over to the moment.

To him.

To the wild sensations that were racing pell-mell through her.

She'd suspected it would be like this, a wild tangling of bodies unlike anything she'd ever known. She'd had no idea, though, that it would be more.

So much more that she wasn't sure if she could stand it. If she was equipped to stand it. Even happiness had to be consumed in finite doses.

She was going to regret crawling out on this limb,

she knew that. It was as certain as the sun rising again tomorrow. But she didn't care.

All she wanted was to feel like a woman.

His woman.

Heaven help her, she'd lost her mind. And she didn't care.

He had held himself in check far longer than he'd thought humanly possible. His hands played along MacKenzie's body as if she were a fine instrument, touching her everywhere. And each new slope, each new peak that he explored made her twist and turn into him. Made her moan as an urgency to make love seemed to take over her body.

When her fingers urgently cupped him, he nearly gave it up and knew that there was no more holding back. It was no longer humanly possible for him.

Pushing MacKenzie down against the bed, he slid into her, at first gently, then at the last moment, he thrust his pelvis hard.

The rhythm began.

Words bubbled up inside of him. Words that came from nowhere and sought her out as their target. Tender words. Sweet words. Trapped behind his teeth and on his tongue as he struggled to keep from uttering them.

Were they mirrors of the emotions he was feeling? Or born of the moment?

He'd never wanted to tell another woman that he had feelings for her during the act of lovemaking. Not even with the one who had gained his heart.

What was happening to him?

He couldn't spare the time to think, to wonder. An urgency had gripped him, pushing him on faster and faster as MacKenzie moved her hips swiftly and seductively beneath his.

When he reached the peak he sought, a euphoria seized him, holding on so tightly that it slowed his descent. Quade's hammering heart helped decelerate his fall back to earth.

Drawing in a huge breath, feeling shaken to the core, Quade looked down at the woman who had caused him to have this out-of-body experience.

"What the hell just happened here?" he whispered in a voice that threatened to crack if he raised it.

It took her a moment to realize he was talking. Another moment to focus on the words and make sense of them, like small pieces on a Scrabble board that somehow managed to come together.

She took a deep breath, wondering how long it would take her to stop vibrating inside. She wanted to hold on to him forever.

And it frightened her.

Because she knew that "forever" was only a myth for the very innocent. And she wasn't that any longer.

"I'm not sure, but if we could patent it, we would probably both stand to make a great deal of money," she murmured.

Damn, she was making conversation, she upbraided herself. Striving to play down the moment and the wildness that was ricocheting inside of her. While he was still inside her, she realized abruptly.

It was unreal.

And yet, it all felt so natural that it made her ache. Because she wanted it to continue. All this was wrong seven ways from sundown and she still wanted it to continue.

As if reading her thoughts, Quade very gently rolled off her. Then, in a movement that would forever touch her, he reached over to the crumpled sheet that was beside her and pulled it over to cover both of them.

An almost unbearable sweetness ignited within her.

The air seemed to shift within the room. He caught a whiff of her perfume. Muscles tightened within him. Needs began to rebuild at a prodigious rate.

Heaven help him, he wanted to make love with her again.

Quade looked at the woman beside him in wonder, a man fighting his way to the surface before he drowned. "What did you put in those cookies?"

"A lot of chocolate chips, cinnamon and oatmeal." She turned her face toward his. Their breaths mingled. Her pulse went into overtime again. "Nothing that would cover this."

Quade didn't like what he was feeling. Didn't like that he *was* feeling. Missteps became all too possible then.

It had never been easy to reach him where he lived. He kept his emotions in check. There'd been no string of girlfriends before Ellen. He'd been rather surprised by Ellen, by the tenderness he'd felt when he was with her. By the desire to protect, to shield, that she'd evoked in him. When she'd died, he was certain all those feelings had died with her.

Until today, he didn't think he was capable of ever feeling any of those emotions again. And yet, here they were, poking through, trying to emerge.

Trying to take him hostage again.

He knew the end result of that. Had gone through it once and had no desire to ever, ever experience any of that again. It had taken a great deal of time and effort to get his heart back into relative working order. He didn't want to mess with it again.

What he was feeling, what he *thought* he was feeling was just a fluke, a freak of nature, he told himself. Born of loneliness and nothing more.

Somehow he couldn't quite convince himself.

Quade was looking at her as if he were trying to dissect her. He was as shaken up as she was by all this, she realized. Her mouth was suddenly dry and she had no idea what to say. Where to go from here. Should she reassure him that this was just "one of those things" that happened? That she didn't expect anything because it had?

Because that would have been a lie, even as she tried to convince herself of it. A lie because a part of her did expect something, did hope for something. Hurt beyond words by Jeff, it still hadn't managed to kill the optimist within her.

But men didn't like strings, didn't want to feel as if things were expected of them just because they'd made love with you.

Damn it, say something. Say something before he thinks you're mentally perusing bridal catalogs.

And then, suddenly, she was off the hook. At least for the moment.

Someone was knocking on the door.

The second knock was followed up by a woman's voice. It rang clearly even in the bedroom. "Quade, are you in there?"

Quade and MacKenzie looked at one another at the same moment. Aggie? Why was she out there at this hour?

Quade was out of bed and on his feet in less time than it took to contemplate the action. Moving swiftly, he went into the other room and grabbed their scattered clothing from the living-room floor.

Without a word, he tossed her undergarments and street clothes to her, then closed the bedroom door. Aggie was knocking a third time as he hurried into his jeans and then his shirt. He stuffed his briefs into his pocket and belatedly realized that he was barefoot. The woman probably wouldn't even notice.

Taking a deep breath, he centered himself. The spell that MacKenzie had intentionally or unintentionally cast over him was hard to shake.

"Hang on," he called out. The moment he opened the door, Aggie came sailing in like the Queen Mary II docking in the harbor. There was a newspaper clutched in her hand.

"Have you seen MacKenzie?" she asked. "Her car's parked here, but she doesn't seem to be answering her door."

He was about to tell the woman that he didn't know where MacKenzie was when he heard a flushing sound coming from his bathroom. The next moment, MacKenzie walked out into the living room, beaming broadly.

"That's because she's here," he told Aggie, trying his level best to sound disinterested and not as if his very blood had crept up to the boiling point around the other woman.

"Hi," MacKenzie greeted Aggie affectionately, pressing a kiss to the woman's soft cheek. "Where have you been?" she asked, employing a maneuver her father had once taught her. When in doubt, go on the offensive rather than just defending your own line in the sand. Being on the defensive unexpectedly tended to confuse the other party. "I was looking for you earlier." She gestured toward the plate of cookies that was still on the coffee table. "I wanted to give you some of the cookies I made. When you weren't home, I came to offer some to Quade and wound up staying to help him unpack."

There, MacKenzie silently congratulated herself. She'd covered all the bases. She just hoped that she didn't look as flushed as she felt.

Aggie picked up a cookie and sampled it. She nodded her approval immediately.

"Heavenly," she pronounced. Her eyes fluttered shut for a second as she savored the taste of the cookie before finally continuing. "I came looking for you to show you both this." She thrust the newspaper section toward Quade. It was the section that was strictly devoted to entertainment. She had it folded to the page she wanted them to read. "It's under 'But That's Just My Opinion,'" she prompted.

Taking the paper from her, Quade scanned the page. MacKenzie looked at it around his arm and found the article first. There was even a small photo of Aggie at the bottom.

"There." She pointed to the third column.

"Read it out loud," Aggie instructed after he had begun reading it to himself.

Quade passed the section to MacKenzie. "You do it," he told her. When she raised her eyebrow, he added, "I'm not much on reading out loud."

"We're going to have to work on your speech," MacKenzie said with a shake of her head. She could feel Aggie watching her expectantly. She began reading: "I don't usually stop at the Laugh-Inn for my nightly dose of entertainment, but someone twisted my arm this time and I'm glad they did. Amid the painfully meager talent which we won't go into here because we're merciful, a shining light struggled to emerge the other night. Agnes Bankhead, known as Aggie to her friends—and we all want to be her friends—is a talent to watch. And guess what, folks? She's old enough to be your grandmother. But that doesn't stop this lady. My prediction, she's going to go to the top. And take us with her, laughing all the way. If the manager of that club has any smarts, he'll hire her on as a regular. But that's just my opinion."

Aggie was fairly beaming as MacKenzie handed the newspaper back to her. The woman almost looked like a young girl, MacKenzie thought. "I guess that means that I've got a shot at it."

Quade looked at her for a long moment, welcoming the opportunity to focus on something other than what had just happened in his bedroom. "I don't think you ever doubted that."

And then he smiled at the older woman. It was a soft, gentle smile that instantly transformed him from the brooding man he appeared to be to something far more kind.

To the man she'd made love with less than ten minutes ago, MacKenzie thought. Her heart quickened as moments came back to her. She banked them down before the rising heat had a chance to take hold again and color her cheeks.

"No, not really," Aggie confessed without either false modesty or vanity. She raised her chin, a woman who had conquered the first step of a long journey, infused with the confidence to continue. "Well, I just wanted to share the good news with you two, seeing as how I dragged you both down there to be my support group."

Humor shone in her eyes as they swept over both of them. MacKenzie thought it was her imagination, but she could have sworn she saw Aggie's eyes twinkling as the woman announced, "And now I'll leave you two to your unpacking."

Feeling suddenly fidgety, MacKenzie picked up the plate she'd brought and urged it on Aggie. "Take some more cookies."

"She made enough for two armies," Quade added.

Aggie took five and slipped them into the oversize pocket of the smock she had on. "This'll do me fine," she told MacKenzie when the latter tried to give her a few more. Reaching the front door, she stopped and leaned her head back toward MacKenzie who was directly behind her. "By the way," she whispered, "you missed a button. Hot work, unpacking," she commented.

And then, with a wink, the woman was gone, leaving MacKenzie staring at the closed door.

MacKenzie whirled around on her heel the second the door was shut. The temperature in the room had gone up at least fifteen degrees.

As had her body temperature.

She turned so quickly, three of the cookies went sliding off the plate. Quade was beside her in beat, picking them up.

"Three-second rule," she called out.

All three cookies in his hand, he looked at her as if she'd began spouting gibberish. "Excuse me?"

"Haven't you ever heard of the three-second rule? If something falls on the floor and you pick it up before three seconds, it's okay to eat."

"And the scientific basis for that is that it takes germs three seconds to become aware that there's something on the floor for them to contaminate?"

To his surprise, she flashed a grin. "Something like that."

"I'll have to tell them that at the lab."

"Speaking of the lab, how's the speech coming?" she pressed again.

He'd really left himself open with that one, he thought. "It's not," he told her darkly, setting the plate on the kitchen table.

"Would you like me to help you?"

He looked at her incredulously. The woman was as unscientific as cotton candy.

"What, write it?"

Was he so quick to forget? She'd already volunteered

more than once. "No, but I could be your cheering section and your sounding board."

"You don't know the first thing about the topic."

"Sounding boards don't have to know anything about the topic they're listening to. Their function is to echo back so that the person doing the talking can hear how it sounds."

She almost had him believing what she was saying. What kind of witch was she, anyway? Making him feel things he didn't want to, urging him on to do things he had absolutely no inclination of doing.

"Tell you what," she decided, "we'll postpone unpacking. This is more important."

"It's late."

"The pen and paper won't know the difference."

He was about to comment on the absurdity of what she'd just said when he replayed the words in his mind. His eyes narrowed. "How did you know I use a pen and paper to write instead of a computer?"

For one thing, she hadn't seen one in the apartment yet. For another, he struck her as someone who liked dealing with the uncomplicated basics in life. That meant no computers if he could possibly help it.

"Just a lucky guess. C'mon, no more procrastinating." Hands at his back, she urged him on to the kitchen table, then turned up the light. "You need to get a start."

As usual, arguing with her was useless. He didn't even try.

Chapter Thirteen

She was nothing like Ellen, he thought, once more coming to the end of the speech that he'd been running through his head. The two women were as different as night and day.

Ellen had been quiet, introspective. A perfect match for his own personality. MacKenzie, on the other hand, was a live wire. A vivacious little ball of fire that had captured his attention no matter how much he'd tried to ignore her.

And now, he caught himself watching for her. Found a smile creeping onto his lips in unguarded moments, when thoughts of her would come bursting upon his brain like Fourth of July fireworks suddenly lighting up a pitch-black sky.

He didn't want this.

And yet, he did.

He sighed, sitting back in his chair, rubbing the bridge of his nose. Wishing he could do the same to the tumultuous thoughts in his head. When he'd finally pulled himself together after Ellen's death, the plan had been to lead a quiet, solitary life, doing research. Eat, sleep and work—he'd put nothing more on his life's agenda. Companionship, relationships, love, those were all things that he'd felt were in his past, not to be experienced again.

But MacKenzie had made him realize that as self-contained as he told himself he was, there was a part of him that missed being involved in something greater than himself. Missed hearing voices other than his own in the apartment.

At one point, after she had tried to prepare him for his upcoming speech, he'd told MacKenzie that he missed peace and quiet. But the truth was, not so much. Not when peace and quiet meant a lack of her.

His hand dropped to his side and he straightened, sitting dead still as the import of the thought hit him right between the eyes.

Dear God, when had it happened?

Between work, hand-holding a septuagenarian's budding ego and writing a speech he didn't want to deliver, when had he had time to start caring about MacKenzie?

When had he started caring again?

He didn't have time for this, Quade told himself as annoyance took hold. Didn't have the stamina for this. Because "this" meant putting himself out on a limb. A limb that could break beneath him without any warning and send him plummeting back into the abyss he'd been living in before MacKenzie came into his life.

Been there, done that. Didn't want a repeat perfor-
mance.

"Earth to Quade."

Blinking, he realized that MacKenzie was waving
her hand in front of him, trying to get his attention. He
was dazed because what was happening to him was
completely unexpected.

He pushed aside the pages of his speech that sat in
front of him on the table. They slipped to the floor.
"Sorry," he murmured.

MacKenzie picked them up before he had a chance
to. "Little mental vacation there?" she teased. She
placed the pages back on the table. "You know, I'm getting used to that."

At her insistence, he'd been rehearsing the speech
every night after work for five days now. And she had
been there every night to make sure he did. He should
have resented that. So why didn't he?

"It's the only way I seem to be able to find any peace
and quiet," he told her.

Her mouth curved in a smile he couldn't begin to in-
terpret, only that it was so typically her. "You sleep,
don't you?"

"Not when you're in my bed."

That was another thing that had happened as naturally as breathing. In one week's time, as he struggled
with the speech he was honor bound to deliver, they had
become lovers.

Lovers.

He didn't know how else to refer to it, even though
the term brought a tightness to his chest at the same time

it made his heart glad. Each evening she'd come over to help him pull his thoughts together and then had done her best to pull them apart with her sweet mouth and that body of hers that made his own respond in ways he hadn't thought possible.

MacKenzie grinned up at him, her eyes dancing, teasing him. Wreaking havoc with his discipline. "Well, when you 'sleep' with someone, the intention is not to really 'sleep' with them." She used her fingers as quotation marks to offset the second use of the word. And then she looked at him pointedly. "Unless, of course, you're very, very comfortable around them."

For one reason or another, she made his pulse race every time he was with her. That, too, was not business as usual for him. Pulses didn't race, they just beat. Unless MacKenzie was in close proximity.

"Does anyone ever really get comfortable around you? It's like getting comfortable around a shack located in the Mojave Desert filled with explosives. You just don't know if the sun's going to make things so hot that something'll suddenly go off."

She gave him a funny look. "I think I'm going to have to chew on that one for a while. I'm not sure if it's a compliment or not."

He shrugged matter-of-factly. "Just stating a fact of life."

Her eyes met his and she felt something begin to stir inside. Again. The spark went beyond the fierce physical attraction she experienced, the attraction that only increased each time they were together. Something about Quade compelled her to seek him out.

Most of all, she wanted to make the sadness in his eyes go away.

Right. And that'll go right after you tell him that you're pregnant with someone else's baby.

Rising from the table, MacKenzie stretched. Restless. This didn't have a prayer of going anywhere and she knew it, but she just couldn't make herself get off the ride. She knew it was because she was weak. Because she wanted to savor the sensations he created within her just a little longer.

She forced herself to get back to business. "Okay, Doctor, from the top. One more time." She laughed when he groaned. "Hey, the moment of truth is tomorrow. You need to be ready. Aggie doesn't leave anything to chance before she goes on." She nailed him with a penetrating look. "Are you going to tell me that you're less prepared than a seventy-two-year-old woman?"

He was tired of the speech. Tired of everything. Except for her. "No, I'm going to tell you that you're a slave driver."

She grinned more broadly. "No argument." And then, like a drill sergeant, she tapped the pages on the kitchen table and issued an order. "Now, from the top."

"As you wish."

A whimsy came over him. Maybe he'd gone over the edge, he didn't know. He was too tired to analyze it. Instead of beginning to recite the speech that was all but embossed on his mind, he caught her up in his arms and began to kiss her.

A squeal of surprise escaped her lips before she sank into the kiss. Then, laughing, suspended three inches off the ground, MacKenzie braced her hands against his shoulders and created a space between them. "What do you think you're doing?"

"Starting from the top, like you told me." A look MacKenzie could only describe as mischievous entered his eyes. Holding her by the waist, he gave a jerk of his wrists and moved his hands to her hips, raising her higher. Tantalizing her. "Of course I could always start at the bottom."

Still holding her, he slowly slid her down along the length of him. A sigh of surrender escaped her lips. It was all the incentive he needed. The smile that bloomed in her eyes pushed him over.

MacKenzie laced her fingers around his neck. "You're bad," she told him.

She'd tapped into all sorts of things he hadn't thought existed within him. "And who made me that way?"

He watched a knowing look enter her eyes. "I beg to differ. You're too strong willed for anyone to make you do anything you didn't want to do."

She had his number, he thought, but he wasn't going to explore that now. Now all he wanted to do was forget that he was going to be standing up in front of a room full of wealthy strangers, delivering a speech that still clung to the roof of his mouth every time he thought about giving it.

He wanted to just lose himself in her.

His mouth met hers and the rest unfolded as naturally as breathing. As naturally and as wondrously as the sunrise that occurred each morning, but was still something magnificent to behold.

She was a force of nature to be reckoned with, he thought. And savored.

MacKenzie wiggled as he undressed her. Wiggled so that her body teased his, making him hard even before he could get her nude. He wanted to linger over every part of her, to savor her, but she always caused his blood to rush madly through his veins, bringing with it an urgency he was still completely unaccustomed to.

She was, for him, the personification of excitement. Familiar, yet different each time he took her.

"This really isn't the way to practice your speech," she told him even as she yanked away his shirt and then made short work of his jeans.

Instead of answering, he caught her to him, savaging her mouth, savoring the taste at the hollow of her throat. Wondering if there was some kind of a scientific term for the madness that seized him every time they made love.

"No," he finally managed to agree, his breath already growing short, his patience shorter, "it's a way to forget about it."

He swept aside the pages on the table, sending them to the floor again. And then, he raised her up onto the table and sheathed himself in her. The look in her eyes drove him on. A madness throbbed in his veins, in his loins. The explosion came quickly for both of them.

The next moment, spent, still joined, he pulled her up so that he could take her back into his arms. So that he could kiss her because the mere act was not enough. He wanted to taste her, to smell her as the euphoria overtook him. Because she was becoming as much a part of him as his own skin.

Clinging to him, she could hardly catch her breath. "That's a hell of an opener," she said, her voice husky. "What are you going to do for a closer?"

He laughed then, the sound undulating into her very being. And then a seriousness came over his features. "I'll show you."

Picking her up into his arms, he carried her to his bed.

There were no more rehearsals that night. He was letter perfect.

MacKenzie chewed on her bottom lip as she slowly turned around in front of her full-length mirror, critically looking at herself from all angles. Wondering if she had made the right choice.

Wondering if she had time to change into yet another dress one last time.

Her bed and the floor around it were littered with dresses she'd tried on and discarded. A score of evening dresses she had either recently bought, borrowed or owned had all been subjected to intense scrutiny and for the most part, found to be lacking for one reason or another.

It didn't help that her favorite dress, a sparkly royal blue gown, felt as if it were tight on her. Reminding her of her pending state. And the fact that she was still keeping it a secret from Quade. A secret because she knew in her heart that once she told him, it would cause this wonderful ride to come to a grinding halt. Her secret would end this special bond between them.

Quade wasn't looking for a long-term relationship. Springing a child on him would be the catalyst he'd need to end things.

How had this happened? she wondered. How had she managed to fall into a trap she'd sworn she'd never revisit? What was she, a glutton for punishment?

No, just a woman who had fallen in love with a man who didn't want to be loved.

She looked at the reflection in her mirror. Tonight was about him. About the work he did and the money that was going to be raised because of all the people Dakota knew. Tomorrow was soon enough to get maudlin, she told herself sternly.

The doorbell rang, sending her heart racing up into her throat.

So much for changing again. She was just going to have to hope that this would do.

Picking up her silver evening bag, she walked into the living room just as the doorbell pealed again.

"Coming," she called out.

She glanced down at her gown, smoothing it one last time. The butterflies were gathering on the runway. She hoped they wouldn't make things too uncomfortable for her baby.

Bracing herself, pasting a smile to her lips, MacKenzie opened the door.

The look in Quade's eyes chased all the butterflies away. For a fleeting moment, she felt as if he were visually making love to her.

She'd chosen wisely after all, she congratulated herself.

The winning selection was a floor-length, slender red dress that had made itself intimately familiar with every contour of her body. Slit up to her upper thigh, the edges flirted with her legs with every step she took, turning every movement into a symphony of seduction. The dress had a high neckline that drew the eye to her bare shoulders. The back plunged down to her waist.

MacKenzie focused her attention on Quade. He was dashing in his tuxedo. She knew that if she said as much, it would probably annoy him and he was undoubtedly nervous enough.

So she couched her approval in more neutral, acceptable language he could live with. "You clean up nicely."

Quade hardly heard her. His attention was riveted to the way the clingy material molded itself to her body. For two cents, he'd stay there tonight and make love with her until they both expired. It was far more appealing than standing up in front of a crowd, trying to expel words from a bone-dry mouth.

It's for a good cause, he reminded himself. His body wasn't so certain. "I was just thinking the same thing about you," he told her.

She laughed, knowing that for him he'd paid her a heady compliment. "Thank you. Are you ready?"

He knew she was asking about the speech. She wanted to know if he felt prepared. And he didn't. The hug knots in his stomach weren't going to go until after the speech was over.

"No," he told her honestly.

She felt for him. The last two go-rounds had been flawless, but that was because he'd delivered the speech to her. What if he came down with stage fright? In a way, it would be all her fault, because she'd been the one to get the ball rolling in the first place.

"During your speech, if you get stuck, just look at

me," she urged. "I know your speech backwards and forwards. I'll prompt you."

He blew out a breath, annoyed at feeling this unsettled. After all, it was only a speech, not mortal combat. Somehow, that had no impact. "Forward would be nice."

She grinned, picking up her wrap from the back of the chair. "Okay, forward it is. Remember, look for me. I'll be the one in red."

Right, like he'd have trouble locating her, especially considering what she was wearing.

"No way I could miss you." Taking the wrap from her hands, he placed it about her shoulders. His hands lingered just a moment before he withdrew them. "Neither could anyone else." He was acutely aware of the bare back beneath the silver shawl. Acutely aware of his body reacting to her. "I could recite the alphabet tonight and no one would be the wiser. Everyone's going to be staring at you."

She looked at him over her shoulder. "They've seen a red dress before."

It wasn't the dress, it was the woman in the dress. "Not like this they haven't."

Moved, she turned around and brushed her lips against his quickly. Softly. "That's the sweetest thing you've ever said to me."

A woman needed to hear things, he thought. And for the most part, he wasn't very good at that. "I guess I'd better brush up on that, too."

That the thought even crossed Quade's mind moved her beyond description. MacKenzie touched his cheek, feeling things within herself that were so impossibly bittersweet, she could have never put them into words, not even if she lived forever.

"Don't change a hair for me," she told him. Taking a deep breath, she slipped her arm through his. "Now let's go and raise that money."

"I just want to get this speech over with."

Shutting the door, she locked it, then tossed the key into her purse. "That, too."

It was the largest affair he'd ever attended. At first glance, the ballroom that had been reserved for that evening appeared endless. The functions he'd gone to while working in Chicago had been small and, for the most part, forced upon him. He didn't socialize well.

As if sensing this, MacKenzie, he noted, never left his side, even though several times during the evening, people attempted to draw her away. She staunchly remained with him. Silently offering her support.

When it came time to deliver his speech, he did better because of her. Following her last-minute suggestion, he gave the speech to her as he had a dozen times before.

It went well. Even he thought so.

Scores of people came up to him afterward with comments and questions. He fielded them all. Even then, MacKenzie remained at his side, content to play a secondary role to his. Looking proud of him.

Was this what contentment felt like? He wasn't sure, but he was willing to find out.

"I knew you had it in you." Adam Petrocelli had been one of the first to congratulate him once the speech was over. "And this crowd—I don't know how you managed it, but Wiley Labs knows how to make its gratitude known," he promised.

"I had very little to do with it," Quade told him honestly.

It was the only time that MacKenzie interrupted that evening. "Don't listen to him. He's exceptionally modest."

"So I'm beginning to see." And then Petrocelli's attention was taken by a celebrity he wanted to meet and he hurriedly excused himself.

For Quade's part, he'd never seen so many celebrities before. Of course, if it hadn't been for MacKenzie at his side, prompting him with names he was only marginally familiar with, he wouldn't have known that half of these people *were* celebrities.

They had all been corralled by Dakota, who periodically would pop up, bringing him people to meet. Generous people, it turned out, who wanted to lighten their guilt at being paid impossibly huge sums of money.

He watched and listened in disbelief as the coffers of Wiley Laboratories swelled during the course of the evening to what seemed like the near-bursting point. By evening's end, if only half the pledges that had been given were honored, the fate of the research facility was secured for at least the coming decade, if not longer.

They remained until the last person had left the gala. Feeling exhausted but exhilarated, Quade drove home and brought MacKenzie to his apartment rather than her own, silently telling her that he wanted her to stay the night.

The thrill she felt was tempered with nerves.

"How does one person know that many people?" he asked as they walked into his living room.

MacKenzie kicked off her shoes even before Quade shut the door.

"Geometric progression," she replied simply. She saw him raise a skeptical eyebrow. "Okay, think of it in terms of spreading a communicable disease, except in this case, that 'disease' is friendship. One person sneezes in a crowd. That crowd goes on to interact with small spheres of their own. By nightfall, you've got yourself an epidemic. Except in Dakota's case, it's more like a lovefest."

She tossed her wrap and purse onto the chair, making a mental note to do something special for her friend. Good cause or not, Dakota didn't have to do this. "Never met anyone who didn't like her or could say no to her."

"You have that in common then." She looked at him quizzically and he explained. "People don't say no to you, either."

MacKenzie laughed. She wasn't nearly as charismatic as Dakota was. "You'd be surprised."

"Yes, I would be." He felt far too wound up to go to sleep. He crossed to the kitchen and opened the refrigerator. "I'm having some wine. Would you like something to drink?"

"Just soda if you have it."

At the fund-raiser, he'd noticed that MacKenzie had only had bottled water. "Don't you ever drink anything alcoholic?" It was just a throwaway question, born of curiosity.

He had given her the perfect opening. A way to finally get rid of the guilt she was carrying around, the guilt that grew every day until it weighed too heavily on her shoulders. Panic pricked at her, but she pushed it aside. She had to do the right thing.

MacKenzie took a breath, then said, "I used to."

He took a glass out for himself and then one for her soda. "But?"

She curled her fingernails into the palms of her hand. "But that was before I found out I was pregnant."

The second glass slipped from his fingers, hitting the sink. The sound of glass meeting porcelain embedded itself into the vibrating silence, splintering it.

Chapter Fourteen

Quade kept his back to her. She saw it stiffen as her words sank in.

"Is it mine?"

His tone was so devoid of emotion she didn't know if he would welcome a denial or become angry because of it. But it didn't matter—she couldn't lie to him. Even though to murmur *yes* would have been the simplest way out for her. His actions if he believed he was the baby's father would allow her to gauge if he had feelings for her.

She was confident he was a decent man. That if there was a child bearing his genes, he would do right by it. Maybe he would even stay with her, even—

What was she thinking? As much as she realized that she wanted him, she didn't want him that way. Not imprisoned by lies.

The true measure of the man was going to be by what he would say when confronted with the truth. That the man who had left her with a broken heart had also left her with something else. Something that couldn't be swept away or mended in time.

If he stood by her then...

There was only one way to find out.

She wrapped her courage around herself and said, "No, it's not."

Quade turned from the sink and looked at her for a long moment, his legs feeling rubbery, as if they would give way at any second.

It was happening again. The foundations of his world were being knocked out without any warning, just as they had been the first time. Everything had seemed right then, too. Had seemed to be going well and then from out of nowhere came a blow that had left him reeling.

"You're sure," he asked, his eyes intent on her face.

Dread drenched her. This wasn't going to turn out well, she could feel it. MacKenzie pressed her lips together and nodded. "I'm sure."

Like a man about to go under for the last time, he grasped at any twig that floated by. "But you could be wrong."

"No," she told him quietly. "I couldn't."

Quade's eyes narrowed as the full weight of her words hit him with an overwhelming force. "The only way you could be sure if—"

She slowly nodded her head, knowing what he was thinking. "I knew I was pregnant when I met you. Yes, I did."

She'd deceived him. By not saying anything, by keeping her condition to herself, she'd deceived him. Deceived him by omission. Deceived him when he would have bet anything in the world that they had an honest relationship. That there wasn't a deceptive bone in her body.

He would have lost that bet, he thought disparagingly.

Quade didn't know what to think, what to feel.

"You knew that you were pregnant with someone else's baby and you still made love with me?"

It was an accusation. She stiffened. "It wasn't something I planned to do."

He no longer knew what to believe. Every word out of her mouth could be a lie. "I don't remember taking you by force."

She felt like screaming, like crying. Like asking him if they could somehow please start over. But the time for all that had past.

"No, not unless you mean by the sheer force of what was happening between us. When you kissed me the way you did, I couldn't think of anything *but* making love with you."

Without realizing it, she wrapped her fingers around the cameo at her throat. Her insides were shaking as she waited for him to say something positive. Something to reassure her that she hadn't just stupidly thrown away this bright, shining chance at happiness that had so unexpectedly fallen into her lap.

No, she hadn't done anything stupid, she insisted fiercely. Stupid would have been to willfully allow Quade to believe this child was his. By telling him the truth, she was preventing future heartache.

Right, and welcoming it now instead.

She blew out a shaky breath, ordering herself not to cry. "I'm telling you now because you have a right to know."

His eyes only darkened at her words. "And I didn't before?"

"That's not what I meant. I didn't know if this—" she gestured helplessly between them "—was going to go anywhere—and I didn't know how to say it."

His expression never changed. She was losing the battle, she thought.

"How about 'I'm pregnant'?"

"And when was I supposed to say it?" she demanded hotly. "When we were talking about the fund-raiser? When we were at Aggie's debut? When?" she wanted to know angrily.

"How about before I made love to you?"

What, it was all one-sided, all male-oriented? Was his ego hurt, was that what this was all about? "You didn't make love *to* me, you made love *with* me. And I was afraid if I said something before, we wouldn't have made love at all and I wanted that more than anything in the world."

She'd said too much, been too honest, she upbraided herself. Why couldn't she just walk away with her dignity intact?

Quade's frown deepened, burrowing through the recesses of his being. Everything she was saying made sense. And yet, none of it made sense. He felt betrayed, cheated and a whole host of things he couldn't even begin to put into words. Most of all, he felt as if his trust had been violated.

"Anything else I should know?" he demanded.

That I love you.

If she listened very hard, she could hear her heart breaking. MacKenzie looked down at the floor.

"No," she answered quietly.

When she raised her eyes again, she saw that Quade was nodding slowly, like a judge debating the sentence he was about to pronounce.

And then they came. The words she didn't want to hear. "Maybe we need to take a break from one another for a while."

If he'd taken a knife and twisted it straight into her heart, it couldn't have hurt her any more.

But if that was the way he felt, there wasn't anything she could do about it. She certainly wasn't going to beg him to change his mind. Beg him to hold her and tell her he wanted her in his life.

With superhuman effort, she forced an indifferent smile to her lips.

"Maybe we should," she echoed. "Whatever you want is fine with me."

She sounded almost relieved to have it over with, Quade thought. At the very least, she was taking it lightly. As if what she'd just said hadn't taken a sledge-hammer to his heart.

With all his being he wished he could be like the other men he knew, men who would have been relieved to hear that they weren't the father of MacKenzie's baby, that they could continue to have a relationship of sorts without strings for a while longer.

But he had never been the kind who welcomed su-perficial encounters, who embraced one-night stands with women whose names and faces faded into the dark. He believed in serious relationships. And Ellen had been his only serious relationship.

Until now.

Except that it apparently wasn't serious, he thought. At least, not to MacKenzie.

He wasn't saying anything. Wasn't trying to talk her out of this. What did she expect?

MacKenzie rose to her feet, slightly surprised that her legs actually supported her. It felt as if everything inside of her was comprised of brittle matchsticks, threatening to break apart at any moment.

"Maybe I'd better go home," she heard herself saying, her voice echoing hollowly in her head.

Not waiting for an answer from him, MacKenzie crossed to the door, then opened it. All the while praying that Quade would do or say something to stop her. Would rush up to her at the last moment, take her hand off the doorknob and turn her around to face him.

When he let her walk out without a word, she knew it was over.

Hand fisted, MacKenzie punched her pillow. How was it that there wasn't a single comfortable shape to be derived from it? She hadn't gotten more than ten hours sleep in the last five days.

A ragged sigh escaped her lips. It was going to be another night spent watching shadows chase each other across her ceiling, courtesy of the tree outside her window. She felt like a card-carrying member of the living dead.

For five days now she'd dragged herself through her life, trying very hard not to show anyone what was going on inside because she wanted no part of answering questions.

Dutifully, she'd reported to Dakota, telling the TV hostess of Quade's gratitude. But when Dakota had attempted to ask her something personal about the man, MacKenzie had become evasive. So much so that Dakota had obviously sensed she needed time to work out whatever was going on and had backed off.

But there wasn't anything going on. Absolutely nothing. That was the whole problem. Her world felt like the aftermath of a nuclear detonation that had wiped out all life-forms on the planet.

MacKenzie punched her pillow again, then deposited her head in the new space. She had to snap out of it, she told herself. This wasn't any good for the baby.

Hell, it wasn't exactly wonderful for her, either, she thought bitterly.

To compound matters, she'd felt like a fugitive, sneaking home every night to avoid running into Quade. Secretly hoping he was waiting to run into her.

MacKenzie moaned. She didn't know how much more she could take.

Flat on her back, she laid her arm across her eyes, closing them. Knowing it would do no good. Everything pointed to her going into work looking like a zombie. Again.

The moment she heard the banging on her front door, MacKenzie popped up in bed like a piece of toast being summarily ejected out of a defective toaster.

Quade.

He'd come to apologize.

But if that was the case, why was he banging on her door as if he meant to take it off the hinges using nothing more than his bare knuckles?

A premonition twisted the pit of her stomach.

Her baby was definitely not getting a smooth ride these days, she thought as she kicked the covers aside and scrambled out of bed. Grabbing her robe, she hurried to the door.

"Who is it?"

"MacKenzie, it's me. Aggie." The woman sounded distressed. "I need help."

Disappointment was immediately shoved aside by concern the moment MacKenzie pulled open her door.

"What's the—?"

She didn't need to complete the question. Aggie was standing before her, holding her beloved pet in her arms. Both she and the Jack Russell terrier had blood smeared over them. A closer look told MacKenzie that the blood was coming from the whimpering animal.

Aggie looked beside herself and for the first time since MacKenzie had met her, the woman actually looked her age.

"Cyrus was attacked," she cried. "I was walking him inside the complex and this big, black dog came running out of nowhere. He lunged for Cyrus, taking him down. I thought he was going to kill Cyrus."

MacKenzie quickly scanned the other woman, but there didn't appear to be any marks on her. "Where's the dog now?"

"I don't know." Aggie shrugged, confused. "I screamed and he ran off." Her voice caught as a sob broke into her narrative. "I need to take Cyrus to the vet, but my car's in the shop."

The dog was whimpering and MacKenzie felt completely helpless. "Oh, Aggie, I'm so sorry. Just let me throw something on and I'll take you."

Even as she talked, she was hurrying into her bedroom. Grabbing a pair of jeans and a sweatshirt, she pulled them on and was out again in less than two minutes. She picked up her purse from the coffee table and checked to see if her car keys were inside. They were. She slung the strap over her shoulder.

"Are you sure the vet's open at this hour?"

"It's a twenty-four-hour emergency clinic," Aggie told her. "Cyrus's vet gave me the address in case I ever needed it. I didn't think I ever would." She didn't bother wiping the tears that came to her eyes. They spilled on the dog she was cradling to her chest. "Please hurry," she begged.

MacKenzie shoved her bare feet into the high heels she'd discarded earlier. The keys were in her hand. "Let's go," she urged.

When she opened the front door, she collided with Quade. His hand was raised to ring the doorbell and he quickly grabbed her by the shoulders to keep her from falling.

Awake, he'd heard the commotion next door. Thinking the worst, he'd come over to see for himself.

"What's going on?" he demanded.

The next moment, looking over MacKenzie's shoulder, he had his answer.

For some reason, she wanted to shove him angrily aside. To tell him to get out of her life. With effort, she held herself in check. This wasn't the time to get into anything.

"Cyrus was attacked," she told him flatly. "I'm taking him and Aggie to an all-night emergency facility. Now if you'll get out of our way—"

But he didn't. There was concern in his eyes as he looked at the dog and the older woman. "We'll take my car," he said stonily. Before MacKenzie could protest, he added, "It's bigger."

He went to take the animal out of Aggie's arms, but Cyrus whimpered so pathetically that Quade withdrew his hands. Instead, he quickly surveyed the nature and extent of the dog's injuries. Cyrus's left ear had been mangled and there were teeth marks along his throat. Most of the blood appeared to be coming from there.

Quade pulled a handkerchief out of his back pocket. "Here." He held it out to Aggie. "It's clean. Hold this to his throat," he ordered. Slipping his arm around Aggie, he guided the older woman to his car. MacKenzie followed immediately behind them. "It's going to be all right," he told Aggie in an authoritative voice.

It was what Aggie needed to hear, MacKenzie thought. She could tell the woman was clinging to Quade's promise. After all, he was a doctor. That meant the promise carried weight.

Holding the rear passenger door open, he helped Aggie and her injured pet inside. Very carefully, he strapped them in as tenderly as if he were strapping in a child. Once that was done, he hurried into the driver's seat and put on his seat belt.

"Where's this facility?" he asked.

Aggie gave him the address her vet had given her, then corrected herself when she realized that she'd transposed the numbers. Luckily, it wasn't located too far away.

Traffic at four in the morning in the city was decent. They made good time.

The moment he pulled up before the building, his the only car in the lot except for an old tan Volvo, Quade jumped out of the car and hurried to help Aggie with the animal.

MacKenzie was there ahead of him.

"I've got her," he said, gently elbowing MacKenzie aside. "You ring the bell, tell them we're coming."

This time he took the dog from Aggie. "Careful," she cried.

"I'm being as gentle as I can, Aggie."

She nodded, attempting to force a smile to her lips. "I know you are, dear."

When there was no response after she rang the bell once, MacKenzie resorted to knocking just as Aggie had. The door opened as Quade and Aggie reached the single-story white building.

"He was attacked," Aggie cried. "Can you help him?"

The vet looked at the blood-soaked handkerchief Quade was holding against the dog's neck. "We'll do our best," the man promised. Admitting them into the building, he gestured toward the small foyer. "Wait right here. Julie, I need a gurney."

The next moment, a dark-haired woman in a white

smock came out of the back room, pushing a gurney before her. Very gently, Quade placed Cyrus on the pristine surface. The dog cried again and Aggie pressed her hand to her mouth.

"He's going to be all right," MacKenzie told her, putting her arms around the older woman. "Are you going to operate?" she asked the vet.

"Right away." Picking up a clipboard from the desk, he handed it to Aggie. "Just fill out the information for our files and leave it on the desk here." With that, he pushed the gurney into the back area and disappeared.

Quade moved in front of the vet's assistant, preventing the woman from following. "How long will it take?"

She seemed uncertain. "Might be a couple of hours." There was compassion in her eyes as she looked at Aggie. "You might as well go home. We'll call you when the operation's over."

Quade never hesitated. He knew exactly what Aggie had to be going through. Cyrus was her companion and she loved the small animal. There was no way she would want to wait out his surgery at home, not when it appeared to be so serious.

"We'll wait right here," he told the assistant.

The woman nodded. The next moment, she hurried after the vet, disappearing behind the double doors.

There was no waiting room to speak of. Only the foyer where they had entered. There were a couple of folding chairs leaning against the wall. Quade brought them over, setting them up one at a time.

"Why don't you sit down?" he suggested to Aggie. "It looks like this is going to take a while."

Aggie wrapped her arms around herself, staring at the closed doors. When she made no response, Quade gently guided her to the first chair.

She sat down. Then, as if suddenly aware of her surroundings, she said, "Look, why don't you two go home? I'll be all right here. After the vet talks to me, I can catch a cab."

"Not a chance," Quade told her. He placed his hand on her shoulder and squeezed it. "You don't have to face this alone."

He had no way of knowing how much his simple gesture of kindness moved MacKenzie. "You should take MacKenzie home," Aggie insisted.

"No, he shouldn't," MacKenzie countered. "Besides, I don't have any place to be."

Aggie looked at the large clock that hung on the wall. It was four-twenty. "How about in bed?"

MacKenzie glanced at Quade before answering. "Tossing and turning is getting a bit old. Looks like you're stuck with the two of us."

Aggie's mouth curved in a half smile. "Looks like."

Quade made himself comfortable on the floor next to the chair Aggie had taken. MacKenzie sat down on the chair next to hers.

Aggie placed her hand on Quade's head affectionately. "You two are the best," she told them softly. "I'm not going to forget this. And neither will Cyrus."

"He'll pull through," MacKenzie said again, knowing that it helped to hear reinforcement.

Quade nodded. "He's tough." And then he paused before adding, "Just like Rochester."

"Rochester?" Leaning forward, MacKenzie looked around Aggie.

He'd probably made a mistake, mentioning the animal, but maybe there was no harm in it if it helped pass the time and gave Aggie a little hope. "The Jack Russell terrier I had when I was growing up. Actually, it was a mix, but he looked just like a Jack Russell."

"You had a dog?" MacKenzie echoed incredulously. She couldn't readily picture Quade with a dog.

"Yes," he told her matter-of-factly, "I did." Arms clasped around his knees, he looked at Aggie. "As a matter of fact, when I look at Cyrus, I can sometimes see Rochester. Lately I've been thinking of maybe getting a dog again."

Aggie nodded. "Certainly can't beat them for companionship. Unless, of course, you bring a loved one into the picture."

"Even then," MacKenzie said meaningfully. She was looking at Quade as she said it. And wishing she wasn't feeling what she was.

Chapter Fifteen

"He's going to be all right."

The moment the veterinarian uttered the words to Aggie, MacKenzie gave the woman a heartfelt hug. She could feel tears springing to her eyes.

Looking over Aggie's shoulder, Quade could see the tears shimmering in MacKenzie's eyes. The sight left him mystified.

"Didn't you hear him?" he asked as she released Aggie. "He just said—"

Trying to get a grip, MacKenzie waved Quade's logic away. Men had no clue when it came to women, she thought. "I know what he said."

Quade glanced toward the vet, but the older man merely shook his head indulgently. "Then why are you crying?" Quade pressed

"The female of the species cries when she's happy," Aggie told him. She was drying her own eyes with a wadded-up handkerchief. She clasped the vet's hand. "Thank you, Doctor, thank you."

Dr. Vladimir Brown seemed only too happy to be part of the happy outcome. "He's asleep now and we'd like to keep him here for observation. It's just a formality," he assured Aggie quickly when concern returned to her features.

"I think she'd like to see him," Quade prompted the vet.

Stepping back, the vet opened the door to the rear of the clinic. "Certainly. Right this way."

With his assistant manning the front, Dr. Brown led them all into the back, past the area where emergency surgeries were performed with a fair amount of regularity. A lingering antiseptic odor seemed to cling to the very air as they walked by. The cages where animals were allowed to recover were located directly behind the operating salon.

Cyrus was the lone occupant as all the other cages stood empty. He was sleeping in the center bottom cage. The dog's ear and throat were bandaged. He looked as if he'd been in a war. And lost.

MacKenzie came up beside Aggie and threaded her arms through hers in a show of support and comfort. "We should put a caption under him reading, You Should See The Other Guy."

Aggie smiled and nodded, looking at her four-footed companion. "I think he'd like that." She sighed deeply. "I'm sure his pride was hurt. He thinks of himself as a little tough guy."

As usual, Quade addressed the business end of the details. Turning toward the vet, he asked, "When can she come by and pick him up?"

"In about five, six hours." Dr. Brown looked at Aggie. "We have your number. We'll give you a call when he's ready to go."

"Cyrus," Quade told the vet quietly for Aggie's benefit. "His name is Cyrus."

The man smiled, understanding. "When Cyrus is ready to go," he corrected.

There were fresh tears shining in Aggie's eyes as she nodded.

Quade glanced at his watch. It was almost seven. By the time he brought them home, it would be time for him to get ready to go to the lab. That meant that he would have been up for over twenty-four hours straight. Not unlike the days when he'd pulled long shifts back to back as an intern.

Thanking the vet, Quade turned to the two women. "I'd better get you two back."

MacKenzie looked at her own watch and swallowed a groan. How had it gotten to be so late? She didn't have to be in until ten today, but that meant there was no way she was going to get any rest.

But then, that was all but a foregone conclusion even before Aggie had shown up at her door, she thought, following the woman out of the clinic. Because she was trying not to think about the man walking behind her, she focused her attention on the woman leading the way to Quade's car.

* * *

The short trip back was spent with Aggie vocalizing her gratitude. Her relief over Cyrus's pending recovery had turned into charged, nervous energy. She talked nonstop, which was a good thing because MacKenzie didn't feel like talking at all and apparently neither did Quade.

Aggie was still talking as they got out of Quade's car and walked to their apartments. Aggie's was first and they paused at her door.

"Certainly makes you take a look at your priorities, doesn't it?" she concluded, reaching into her pocket for her key. "Here I was, bent on conquering new fields, determined to become the next comic sensation and neglecting what I had in my own backyard." She shook her head. "I haven't been paying as much attention to Cyrus as I should, but he just went on loving me anyway."

She inserted her key into the lock and opened the door. But instead of going inside, she gazed at the couple who had been there for her in her time of need. Her face softened into an almost beatific smile.

"You just never know, do you? Each of us are only here for a finite time and we should all enjoy each other while we can." Moving forward, she kissed each of them on the cheek. "I don't know what I would have done if you two weren't here." And then, taking a deep breath, she waved them to their individual apartments. "Go back to your lives—I've kept you long enough."

MacKenzie remained where she was. "You'll be okay?" she asked. The woman had been through a great deal and she wasn't exactly young. This was more

Quade's field of expertise than MacKenzie's, but she couldn't help being concerned.

Aggie laughed. Her eyes moved from one to the other, emotions that defied description washing over her face. "I'll be fine." With that, she walked inside her apartment and closed the door.

The moment the door closed, MacKenzie was aware of the stillness in the early morning air. In the distance was the sound of cars, but here, there was none. Awkwardness threatened to settle in, draping itself around her shoulders.

She let out a shaky breath. "Well, I'd better be getting ready," she murmured, moving to her own door. She began fishing through her purse for her keys, deliberately avoiding Quade's eyes.

"She's right, you know."

The sound of his voice rumbled around her, surprising her. Turning, she looked up at him. "About what?"

"About time being finite. About priorities and enjoying one another when we can." He shrugged. "About a lot of things."

Quade shoved his hands into his pockets, wishing he were better at vocalizing his thoughts, his feelings. He felt as clumsy and unequal to the task as a ballet dancer with size-thirteen feet. For the last few days, ever since he'd discovered that MacKenzie was pregnant with another man's child, doubts and questions had been eating away at him.

There was no good way to ask. He decided that all he could do was just to jump in with both feet and put it to her as directly as possible.

"Do you love him?"

The question hit her right between the eyes. She stared at him. "Him? Who?"

Impatience came, dragging uneasiness in its wake. Just how many *him*s were there in her life? "The baby's father."

She could feel every muscle in her body tightening, like an animal preparing for a fight. Except in this case, she wasn't an animal. But this still had the makings of a confrontation.

Her breath grew short as her pulse accelerated. Was he going to pick a fight right here? When she felt so unprepared to defend herself? With effort, she toned down her defensiveness and examined the question before answering. Honesty was her only choice.

MacKenzie raised her chin. "I did. Once."

He could read between the lines when it came to scientific data. When it came to women, he was hopeless. He needed a road map and a compass. But most of all, he needed a guide.

"But not anymore," he pressed.

"No," she replied evenly, "not anymore." Did he want it spelled out in blood? Jeff was in her past. She'd thought, hoped, that *he* was going to be in her present and future. So much for ever getting a job as a fortune teller, she mocked herself.

Her eyes held his, trying to discern what was at the bottom of all this.

His eyes were flat, not giving her a single clue to work with.

"Why?" he wanted to know.

Her temper flared as she threw up her hands and nearly sent her keys flying.

"What do you *want* from me?" she demanded. "Are you trying to get me to say that I stopped loving him because I fell in love with you? Well, I didn't. I stopped loving him before that ever happened. *Before* I ever fell in love with you," she shouted. "There, I said it. I love you. But don't let that get in your way. I won't be bothering you. I didn't bother you now," she pointed out, gathering a full head of steam. "You came over to my place. And I wouldn't have let you take us to the clinic, except that Aggie needed help and…"

He was very, very tempted to stop her mouth the best way he knew how. With his own. But for the time being, he let her vent, knowing it was important for her to have all this out in the open between them. Because secrets would only kill budding, thriving things.

"I know how that is," he said quietly when she paused to catch her breath. Since she didn't appear to know what he was referring to, he elaborated. "Needing help."

MacKenzie continued to stare at him. She could almost physically feel the minutes ticking away and she knew that at least he was going to be late. But she couldn't stop herself. He'd made an admission to her, however abstract, she would have never thought he was capable of making.

"What would you know about it?" she challenged. Emotional eunuchs didn't know they needed help.

His words came out slowly, as if he were carefully measuring each one the way he did the different variables in his experiments.

"I know I need help in forgetting about you." He saw her eyes widen in surprise. "I've been trying, these last few days, but it hasn't been going very well."

She stared at him, stunned. She would have never thought he could make such a confession. Was she just overtired and hallucinating? "Well, don't look at me. You're on your own there."

"Except that I don't want to be." Eroding the distance between them, he took a risk and put his hands on her waist. She didn't shrug him away. It gave him hope. "Being on my own after having someone to love is too empty. Too stark."

He paused, trying to find the words that continued to elude him. It was like playing hide-and-seek with the wind, but he did the best he could. He suddenly realized that if he couldn't make her understand now, he might never get another chance.

He was risking everything.

"After losing Ellen, I never thought that I could ever feel anything again." He drew her in a little closer, doing more with his eyes than with his hands. "That anyone could ever make me feel again. The truth was, I didn't want to find anyone. I was afraid of finding someone." He took a breath. "Now, the only thing I'm more afraid of than finding someone is losing that someone. I've spent these last few days trying to get back to where I was before you bounced into my life—"

"Bounced?" she echoed incredulously.

"You do bounce," he pointed out, his mouth softening as he allowed himself a smile. "There's so much life, so much energy in you, you just bounce into every day.

But I can't get back to where I was," he continued, his eyes serious. "Not with you living next door. Not when I know all I have to do is knock on your door to see you."

His words were giving her hope. But she was afraid to hope. Afraid of walking out on that platform and finding that there was nothing beneath her feet but air. She wasn't some Saturday-morning-cartoon character who could scramble back to safety. She would fall flat on her face.

Her eyes held his as she asked, "So you're telling me you want one of us to move?"

God, communication just *wasn't* his forte. Exasperated, he made it as plain as he could. He bared his soul. "No, I'm telling you that I love you."

She was free-falling, she realized. But definitely *not* like some Saturday-morning cartoon. This was wonderful. There was wind beneath her sails and exhilaration rushing through her.

"Well, then, why didn't you say something? Why didn't you knock?"

There was no point in telling her that he had materialized so quickly outside her door this morning when she was dashing out to take Aggie and Cyrus to the clinic because he'd finally made up his mind to do just that. At four o'clock in the morning, he had come face-to-face with his feelings and decided to do something about them instead of waiting for them to somehow vaporize and leave him alone.

So now he did something he'd never done before in his life.

He pretended.

Quade raised his hand and knocked on an invisible door.

MacKenzie stared at him, a stunned expression on her face. Not quite trusting her own eyes. "What are you doing?"

"Knocking on your door," he told her matter-of-factly. "Aren't you going to answer it? And my question?"

Had she missed something? "What question?"

It was a step that had filled him with fear, with dread. But as he looked into her eyes, he found that it took no effort, no courage at all to ask, "Will you marry me?"

She *couldn't* be hearing him right. "What?"

"Will you marry me?" he repeated, this time with more verve.

It wasn't April 1st, but it had to be a trick. *Oh, please, God, don't let it be a trick.* She could feel her heart begin to hammer wildly.

"You want to marry me."

"I want to marry you."

"Even though I'm pregnant."

"Even though you're pregnant. The way I look at it, I'm getting two for the price of one."

She couldn't believe him. Was still afraid to believe him. Because to believe and then find out otherwise would hurt too much. "You're kidding me."

Quade framed her face with his hands. He was way overdue to leave for work, but none of that held any importance to him, not now. Not until he could make her believe him.

"I have a limited sense of humor. I don't often kid and never about something as serious as this. I want you and I want your baby, MacKenzie. I can't put it any plainer than that."

She said nothing.

Had he read everything wrong? Was he so taken up with the tug-of-war inside of him that he'd misunderstood the way she felt?

There was no graceful way to back out, nor did he want to.

No, she loved him, he knew it, felt it in his bones as it mated with the same feeling within him. But he didn't want to pressure her. If she needed space and time, he could respect that.

Even if it wasn't going to be easy for him. "Look, if you need time…"

She could hear her own words echo in her head as she said them. "What I need is to believe that this is on the level."

He thought for a second. "I know someone with a polygraph machine, I could—"

"Always the man of science." She laughed as the realization that he loved her began to take root. As joy swelled within, she wrapped her arms around him. A feeling of well-being took over every part of her. "You know, the next seventy years are going to be very interesting."

He held her tightly against him. Relief gave way to longing. He was going to call in late and take the morning off now that he had something to celebrate. "Only seventy?"

Her eyes were teasing him. He was going to love getting lost in them, he thought. "For starters. After that, we'll see."

"Sounds good to me," he told her as he brought his mouth down to hers.

Epilogue

"Well, you certainly don't look like a woman who's about to marry a hunky doctor," Dakota said as she walked into her dressing room and found MacKenzie there. "What's the matter?"

MacKenzie frowned. She was still trying to sort out what had happened earlier this morning at the complex manager's office. No matter which way she examined it, it just didn't make any sense.

"You want it alphabetically or chronologically?"

"I want it any way that makes sense."

"Then you're out of luck."

"Give." Gesturing toward the sofa, Dakota sat down next to her. That was when she noticed. "Where's your cameo? Did you give it away already?"

MacKenzie ran her hand over her throat, as if that

could somehow make the cameo materialize. "No, that's just the problem, I didn't. It's missing. I never take it off. But when I looked in the mirror this morning, it wasn't there. I looked all over my apartment and Quade's." She sighed. "Then I went to Aggie's."

"And?"

"Not only is my necklace missing, but so is she."

Dakota stared at her. "Excuse me?"

MacKenzie began at the top. "I rang her bell. When she didn't answer, I got concerned. I thought maybe Cyrus had a relapse or something, so I looked in through the side window. There was no furniture in the apartment."

Surprise was etched on Dakota's face. "She moved out without telling you?"

MacKenzie held up her hand. "Wait, it gets better. I went to ask the complex manager about her and he told me that the apartment's been vacant since January when the college professor moved out."

"What?"

"My sentiments exactly." She felt as if she'd fallen headfirst into the *Twilight Zone*. "He insisted there was no one there." She looked at Dakota. "It's like I'm losing my mind. She was there, Dakota. If it wasn't for Aggie, I'm not sure that Quade and I would even be together. She was the one who really started the ball rolling." And because of her, two hearts were now unbroken.

MacKenzie scrubbed her hands over her face, too confused to form a clear thought. "Why would she just disappear like that? And why would the manager say she was never there?"

Dakota thought of her husband. "Do you have a photo of Aggie? I can ask Ian to look for her. He's in security systems now, but he was a policeman and this would have been right up his alley."

The moment Dakota made the offer, MacKenzie began to rifle through her purse. "All I have is this photo in the article they did on her when she made her debut at the Laugh-Inn. I was going to show it to you. I thought maybe we could have her on the program as a filler."

When she handed the article with its photograph to Dakota, the latter looked and paled.

"What's the matter?"

Dakota stared at the small picture a moment longer before she raised her eyes toward MacKenzie. "Are you sure this is Aggie?"

MacKenzie felt a nervousness slip over her. "Yes, why?"

Dakota took a deep breath and then let it out. Weird, that's what it was. But then, she believed in the legend—maybe this was all part of it. "Because that looks exactly like the woman who sold the cameo to me. The one at that antique shop upstate I told you about. The one that, when I went back to see her, the people who ran the store told me that she'd been buried on the day that I insisted she sold the cameo to me."

MacKenzie remembered Dakota mentioning this. At the time, she'd thought it was just a misunderstanding. Maybe a case of mistaken identity. But now it was taking on an eeriness.

"You're making this up."

"No, I'm not." Things began to fall into place for Dakota. "Think about it," she said. "The cameo is gone and with it, this Aggie woman. And Quade is very much a part of your life."

MacKenzie took back the article and stared at the woman pictured in it. "So what are you saying? That this is all some kind of magic trick?"

"Not magic exactly, but…" Dakota let her voice trail off.

MacKenzie shook her head. "I don't believe in magic." Doubt began to slip in. Quade *had* come into her life the day after she'd received the cameo. "But even if I did… No, no," she backtracked, stopping her thoughts before they could run away with her. "Aggie was real," she insisted. "The woman had a dog. She performed in front of a bunch of people."

Dakota smiled. She'd thought that woman in the shop was real, too, despite evidence to the contrary. "There are more things in heaven and earth, Horatio, than are dreamt of in your philosophy."

MacKenzie sighed and shook her head. "Quoting Shakespeare. Always knew your degree would come in handy for something."

Dakota squeezed her hand. "All that counts is that Quade is real."

Her thoughts began to get carried away. "Oh God, what if—"

But she never got to finish her statement. Dakota was pointing behind her to the open door and smiling.

MacKenzie shifted in her seat and saw Quade standing there. Like a jack-in-the-box, she was on her feet.

She hadn't been able to reach him when she'd found out about Aggie. "I've been trying to call you. What are you doing here?"

He had taken some time off. The fund-raiser had bought him a great deal of goodwill and leeway. "I wanted to make it official, in case you started to have doubts about it."

Before she could ask him what "it" was, he had taken out a small velvet black box from his pocket. Inside was a ring. A cameo encrusted with tiny diamonds.

With Dakota making appropriate noises behind him, he slipped it on MacKenzie's finger. "I know it's not your standard engagement ring but—"

"It's beautiful," she cried, holding it out so that the diamonds caught the light. "And nothing about this whole situation has been 'standard.'"

He took her into his arms, blessing the miracle that had brought her into his life. Because she'd given him a life. "I wouldn't have it any other way."

And neither would she, MacKenzie thought as he kissed her.

* * * * *

If you enjoyed SHE'S HAVING A BABY, you'll love
Marie Ferrarella's next book, which is available
November 2005 from Harlequin NEXT:
STARTING FROM SCRATCH
For a sneak preview, turn the page…

BY HER OWN INNER CLOCK, she was running late.

By everyone else's method of time keeping, she was ahead of schedule. But Elisha Jane Reed had gotten to her present position of senior editor in the exclusive publishing firm of Randolph and Sons by following, to a good extent, Henry David Thoreau's advice about marching to a different drummer. She marched in double time to that drummer so that she could elude his other equally famous phrase, the one about most men leading lives of quiet desperation.

Because the line applied equally, perhaps even more truthfully, to women, as well.

As contemplated by the late nonconformist, desperation came to her only, should she be awake, in the wee hours of the night, when everything bad was magnified by the shadows in the room and everything good was obscured behind the dust motes. It was then that she took stock of her life, measuring it by the old-fashioned standards that refused to die even in this day and age. The standards that had been laid down for all women since Eve had opted for a more extensive wardrobe than just her long hair and a random fig leaf. Namely, a husband and miniature copies or combinations of herself and the man who had won her hand and her heart.

In that column, as far as her life went, there existed nothing except a very large zero. There were no children, no husband, not even an ex-husband buried beneath disparaging rhetoric. As far as she was concerned, marriage was the name of a mythical realm into which she had never traveled, never even been invited to tour.

Desperation of the more common garden variety existed for her by the truckload within the halls of Randolph and Sons. The more familiar desperation, coupled with exasperation, involved deadlines, temperamental and at times overpaid authors, not to mention the constant, daunting influx of market statistics, which, even when good, were never as good as Hayden Randolph, the seventy-five-year-old retired-but-never-quite-out-of-sight head of the publishing company, desired them to be.

The old man was going to be at the party tonight, Elisha thought as she searched in vain for the mate to the diamond stud earring she'd wanted to wear. Despite the retirement party he'd authorized to be thrown for him last year, he had to have his finger in every pie that came out of the Randolph and Sons oven. He didn't trust his own son to preside over the festivities despite his twenty-four years in the business. Tomorrow, Sinclair Jones's latest thriller, *Murder by Moonlight* hit the bookstores. Tonight was the book's coming-out party.

"Come out, come out wherever you are," Elisha coaxed in an impatient, singsong voice. No diamond stud appeared in reply.

The diamond studs were her lucky earrings and, although she wasn't superstitious by nature, the one time she hadn't worn them to one of these affairs, the author's book had sold abysmally. She would not take chances. Someone had once told her that as an editor you were only as good as your author's current book.

Carole Chambers would really love for her not to find her earrings, Elisha thought, taking the wide, rectangular jewelry box and dumping the contents out on the top of the bureau. Carole Chambers was the assistant that Haydon's son Rockefeller had saddled her with a little more than a month ago. She remembered the day well. She thought of it as Black Monday.

"I want you to train her, Elisha. Make her a junior version of you. Not that I expect anyone to ever be as good as you," he'd said to her. "But Dad wants this to happen. So it's either have you train Carole or we kidnap you in the dead of night, whisk you off to some mad scientist's laboratory and have them create several dozen clones in hopes that at least one will be enough like you to satisfy him."

Smiling at the scenario he'd created, Rockefeller Randolph, Rocky to the select few who numbered among his friends, had raised and lowered his eyebrows and rubbed his hands together like the imaginary mad scientist's slightly madder assistant. She'd said yes because what choice did she have?

Elisha sighed in disgust and reached for one of the many pairs of reading glasses she kept scattered throughout her penthouse apartment. She hated needing glasses. Once she could have made out every single detail of the jewelry spread out on the honey-colored bureau. Now entire pieces melded together in a semi-colorful glob. Colors were no longer as intense as they once had been and letters had become black specks on a surface.

Getting older was the pits, she thought as she donned her glasses. She began sorting through the pieces.

Rocky would be there tonight, too. Sitting off in some corner of the room, communing with glass after glass of whatever wine they were going to be serving. Elisha shook her head. He always seemed to shrink to half his lanky size whenever he was in the same room as his father. Rocky was a very talented, sweet man, but he was considerably short on self-confidence, especially whenever his larger-than-life father was anywhere in the vicinity.

"Too bad the man can't stay retired," Elisha murmured. A necklace had formed a threesome with a pair of her dangling earrings. She gave a halfhearted attempt at separating the pieces, then moved them aside.

Rocky had been the one who'd hired her twenty-four years ago. She'd begun as a proofreader for the company and hiring her, she later found out, had been Rocky's first official act for the company.

Because he enjoyed putting his son through hoops, Hayden Randolph had almost un-hired her the very next day in a fit of temper that had had nothing to do with her and everything to do with his wife's discovery of his latest mistress's existence. Rocky had mustered up his courage, intervened on her behalf and she'd been back on the payroll before she'd been every actually removed. She remembered feeling as if she'd been standing up in the front car of a roller coaster as it took its first hill.

The memory came back to her in large, neon lights. She looked up into the oval mirror over the bureau. "God, was that really twenty-four years ago?" It didn't seem possible. "Almost a quarter of a century ago."

Saying the words out loud created a sudden shiver that slid down her Donna Karan-clad back. A quarter of a century made her sound ancient.

A quarter of a century. She doubted Carole Chambers was much older than that.

Without realizing it, Elisha frowned. Carole made her think of Anne Baxter in *All About Eve*. Except that in the movie, Anne Baxter hadn't initially come across as devious. One look into Carole's baby-blue eyes had been all that she'd needed to know that leaving her back exposed to the younger woman would be a fatal mistake. In another life, Elisha had no doubts, Carole Chambers had gotten from place to place by slithering on her belly.

"Finally!"

Feeling every bit as triumphant as a big-game hunter who had bagged the prey he had set out bring down, she held up the diamond stud she'd finally located. Somehow, it had gotten hidden beneath a chunky gold bracelet. Her mood brightened considerably. She pushed her glasses on top of her head.

All in all, she'd only spent a little more than ten minutes searching for the second stud. Not really that much time in the scheme of things, unless you were running on a tight schedule, which she always was. It was her habit to cram as much as she could into each day until it was fairly bursting at the seams.

If she was too busy to take two deep breaths in succession, that left her no time to think thoughts that weren't directly related to work in some fashion.

Which meant that there was no time for the emptiness and sounds of silence to creep in.

Angling her head, watching herself in the mirror, Elisha fastened the second stud into place. A whimsical smile played on her lips.

"If only the other kind of stud was as easy to find." She dropped her hands from her ear and stared at her image in the mirror. "I just said that out loud, didn't I?" She sighed and shook her head. "God, I've got to get myself a pet so at least I can pretend I'm talking to another lifeform instead of just myself. They lock up people who talk to themselves constantly."

Crossing back to her king-size bed, she slipped on the black pumps that she'd left there, then picked up her wrap. It was black, just like her dress. The thought occurred to her that perhaps she should have put on something more festive, but black was slimming and she needed that right now. Somehow or other, five pounds she neither knew nor wanted had decided to make themselves at home on her body. It wasn't the first time. When she'd been younger, dieting had been a matter of closing her eyes and loudly declaring, "Be gone." That and a week of skipping lunches did the trick. Now, skipping food for a month wouldn't bring about the same results. Just acute hunger pangs that could only be dealt with by the massive influx of food.

She was going to have to exercise, Elisha thought. The notion did not make her feel all warm and fuzzy. She didn't like sweating. Besides, where would she find the time? She'd already used up her extra ten minutes for the month looking for her second stud.

Adjusting the wrap around her shoulders, Elisha slowly surveyed herself in the wardrobe mirror that ran from one end of the bedroom wall to the other. The wardrobe mirror gave the illusion that the bedroom was twice as large as it was. Luckily, it didn't have the same effect on her.

"Not bad," she decided. "Maybe even elegant."

The price tag that had been on the outfit was certainly elegant but money had long since ceased to be an object. Her job paid very well and her needs, other than a centrally located Manhattan apartment, were reasonable and few. She didn't even take long vacations anymore to recharge the way she once had because now it was work, not downtime, that recharged her batteries.

Besides, vacations somehow seemed to underscore the fact that there was no one in her life to share a sunset with now that she was no longer half a couple. She hadn't been since she and Garry had gone their separate ways. She to her work and he to the arms of some tight-skinned, nubile size four named Kelly. Kelly, it had turned out, was exactly the same chronological age as some of his ties.

Elisha picked up her clutch purse from the coffee table and took out her key. A bitter taste rose inside her mouth. It always did when she thought about Garry Smallwood.

There had been a time, in the beginning, when she'd thought that she and Garry might wind up facing eternity together. But as time had progressed, the fabric of that belief had begun to dissolve until it was completely gone. She'd given Garry seven of the best years of her life and he had given her a migraine headache—her first—that had lasted three days when he'd left.

That had been six years ago.

"You're dwelling much too much in the past, 'Lise," she berated herself. She glanced at the reflection in the mirror on the wall opposite the front door. A corner of her mouth rose slightly. "Maybe that's because in the past, you had less skin."

For a second, she was tempted, but then resisted. She wasn't going to get caught up in that, wasn't going to place her fingertips along her cheekbones and push up, ever so slightly, the way she'd once seen her mother do. Her mother had been contemplating a face-lift at the time. Her father had come up behind her, kissed the back of her neck and declared that she wasn't to change anything about the woman he loved.

Elisha sighed. They didn't make men like that anymore, men who loved you and your extra skin. And she, she reminded herself, had made her peace with that. She had a perfectly good life that a lot of people would kill for.

People like Carole Chambers.

If she didn't hurry, the little scheming witch would get there ahead of her, she thought.

SPECIAL EDITION™

presents

the first book in a heartwarming
new series by

Kristin Hardy

Because there's
no place like home
for the holidays…

WHERE THERE'S SMOKE

(November 2005, SE#1720)

Sloane Hillyard took a very personal interest in her
work inventing fire safety equipment—after all, her
firefighter brother had died in the line of duty. And
when Boston fire captain Nick Trask signed up to
test her inventions, things got even more personal…
their mutual attraction set off alarms. But could
Sloane trust her heart to a man who risked his
life and limb day in and day out?

Available November 2005 at your favorite retail outlet.

Where love comes alive™

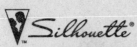

COMING NEXT MONTH

SSECNM1005